FINALE

THE ADAM BLACK THRILLERS #BOOK 5

KARL HILL

First published in 2022 by Bloodhound Books.

www.bloodhoundbooks.com

Print ISBN 978-1-914614-99-6

ALSO BY KARL HILL

THE ADAM BLACK THRILLERS

Unleashed (Book 1)

Violation (Book 2)

Venomous (Book 3)

Fury (Book 4)

1

The process was simple and relatively inexpensive. Essentially, there were four stages once they'd set foot on British soil.

Stage one. The captain of the boat – a Spaniard called Alessandro Abasolo – arranged for them to be deposited on the south coast of England. The locations varied every month, for obvious reasons. His boat was small enough to avoid detection, both from the Coast Guard, and right-wing migrant hunters. The numbers transported were always minimal. No more than six. No less than four. That way, containment was easier to handle. The captain got paid. Twice. By the passengers, in the first instance, for the boat trip. And then by the Syndicate – four thousand a head. Small change, in the great scheme of things. But enough for him to take the risk.

Stage two. Two cars would pick them up. Vans were a no-go. Vans were too obvious. Two average saloon cars however... Haytham Bustan smiled as he reflected on that particular element of the process. His idea, and, in his opinion, one of sheer genius.

Two saloon cars attracted zero attention. Maybe a year old.

Nothing too upmarket. One passenger in the front, two in the back. A family day out, at first glance. And it was the *first* glance which counted. Then, a journey to discreet locations in the north of England. Again, the locations varied month to month. Sometimes a roadside café. Sometimes a supermarket car park. Maybe a lay-by on a country road. Anywhere at all. As long as it changed, and as long as it was ordinary. And as long as there was no CCTV.

Stage three. They were transferred into different cars, same type – nondescript, average – and brought to the rented tenement flat in an area of Glasgow called Govanhill. An area categorised by the government as a placement for asylum seekers. Which fitted in well with the process.

And so stage four. Bustan sat on a leather chair in a corner of the living room. There were no ornaments, the walls bare, the furniture basic. Two couches faced him, with a low coffee table in between, upon which, a saucer adapted as an ashtray. Those who sat opposite had been given sandwiches, and bottles of water. The kids got lemonade and chocolate bars. They each carried a small vanity case with their belongings. Never much, thought Bustan, as he regarded the six people sitting huddled on the couches, staring back at him with wide hopeful eyes. Always hopeful. A hope that shone. Who could blame them, he thought, when you considered the countries they had left behind.

He smiled. They smiled back. They said nothing. Respectful. Six people. A family, he had been told. Mother, father, two teenage sons, a girl of eleven, and the youngest, an eight-year-old boy. The beginning of a new and wonderful life. Bustan took a deep drag of his cigarette – a Capstan, unfiltered – and stubbed it out on the saucer.

A man entered. Bustan began his speech. The man interpreted.

"Welcome to Scotland," Bustan began, as he always did. He had perfected his little initiation over many months. "You've arrived, and now you can at last feel safe, and enjoy life. Relax a little. The worst is over. Your troubles are behind you. Here, you will be protected. We will take care of everything. We will make the applications for asylum. We'll do all the paperwork. You'll have nothing to worry about. Soon, we'll find you accommodation. And schooling. And jobs. Everything will be fine. And no more money. You've paid enough already. From now on, everything is free."

The father – a man of forty, but who looked much older – spoke in faltering English.

"Thank you. Thank you so much. You have been so... kind."

"It's what we do," replied Bustan. "No need to thank me. After what you and your family have been through. We're here to help."

The interpreter relayed the words in fluent Arabic, causing them to smile and nod.

"There is one thing you have to do," continued Bustan, his voice deep, well practised. The voice of reassurance. "It's routine. It's good. We need to take you to a doctor in a hospital. To give each of you check-ups. Yes? To keep you healthy. All normal. All good. For the children."

The interpreter spoke in a low monotone. When he'd finished, the mother clapped her hands. "Yes!" she said. "Doctor good."

"Yes," responded Bustan. "Doctor good."

A half-hour later, a people carrier arrived, tinted windows, unobtrusive, to take them to a private hospital twenty-five miles down the M77, set in woodland on the outskirts of Troon. A seaside town, rarefied and ancient, known throughout the world for its championship golf courses. But there was always shadow in the sunlight, mused Bustan.

He watched them go from the lounge window of the flat, then made the call. It was picked up instantly. "They've left."

"And we're expecting six?"

"Yes. Four children, two adults."

"We'll be waiting."

Bustan gave a rumbling chuckle. "Be sure to give them a nice welcome."

The line went dead. Bustan shrugged. When such calls were made, there were few pleasantries. He couldn't have cared less. In Bustan's world, money was the only thing that mattered, and the Remus Syndicate were exceptionally good payers. In six weeks' time, a briefcase would be delivered to another address, and in it, £240,000. Hard cash. Forty grand a head. He knew the hospital would collect far more. He could ask for a bigger slice, but Bustan knew they'd only go to the next guy. Anyway, it was easy work.

He turned to the interpreter – an old friend from Istanbul called Mehmet Aksoy – and offered him a cigarette. Aksoy nodded, prised one from the packet. He had his own lighter. Bustan popped another in his mouth, lit up. He'd started smoking when he was twelve, and wasn't intending to give up any time soon.

"They always leave with smiles," said Aksoy.

Bustan took a deep drag, contemplated the remark.

"So they should. To them I'm... God."

The edges of Aksoy's mouth twitched into something approaching a smile. Blue-grey smoke coiled around him, like serpent's tails.

"A God, you say? Strangest God I've ever met."

"And how many Gods have you met, Mehmet? They come

here, to this little flat, and I give them joy. I give them hope. I do what a God's supposed to do."

"And after they leave this little flat. What then, Bustan?"

"They meet the Devil."

"Ah. The Devil. Yes. But much worse than that, I think."

Bustan nodded solemnly, inhaled, exhaled, smoke blowing out through his nostrils.

"Much worse."

2

Desmond Gallagher tried to run four miles every evening after work. He would admit that perhaps "running" was a misnomer. A shambling jog was more accurate. Sometimes a fast walk. And only during the summer months. It was too cold and dark in the winter.

His route was always the same. From his house – a comfortable detached villa in a hamlet nestled on the outskirts of Glasgow called Thorntonhall – he would take narrow country roads, looping back in a wide circle. He could virtually miss the traffic. Sometimes a tractor would pass him. Or a cyclist.

But he reckoned he was lucky. Where he lived, he was miles from a main road. Which was how he liked it. The peace and quiet allowed him to think. And Desmond Gallagher had a lot to think about.

It was the beginning of July, and the evening was perfect. There was no wind. A stillness had settled. The sky was pale blue and cloudless. It was early evening. He'd just arrived in from work. Another twelve-hour shift. But today was different. Given the events of that particular afternoon, it was perhaps one of the worst days of his life. He readjusted his thoughts. Not "perhaps". A definite. His wife had made chicken and spinach tortellini. Everything fresh. But he had no appetite.

"Can't it wait?" he said, a little sharply. "I need to clear my head." He'd already changed into a Nike top, joggers, and a pair of somewhat battered running shoes. He gave a small apologetic twitch of his shoulders. "Shit day. Sorry."

"Worse than the usual shit?"

"Off the scale. You don't want to know."

She stepped close, and held him. "A problem shared..." she whispered in his ear.

"Not this problem," he whispered back. "No amount of sharing can help. Where's Tony?"

She pulled away, looked at him. "Still in his room. Where else?"

"I'll go up and see him when I get back."

"Speak to me. Tell me what happened."

Desmond's lips curled into a sad droop. "Let me go for a run. Get some fresh air in my lungs. Clear my thoughts. Then I'll tell you. Promise."

She responded with a resigned shrug, heaved a sigh. "I'll be waiting. Don't take too long. No one likes cold pasta. And remember your phone."

He patted the zip pocket on his trousers. He'd learned from bitter experience, the importance of contact. A twisted ankle on a pothole, and then a long painful hobble back home. Never to be repeated.

He left at 7pm precisely. He started his watch. He could do it in under an hour. Just. The village disappeared behind him. On either side, low drystone walls, beyond which, rolling fields and random pockets of trees. Cows watched him dolefully as he jogged by. No aches. No pains. He never understood why people listened to music while they ran. The sound of his own breathing, the pad of his trainers on the asphalt, the chirp of birds, the breeze, the sway of branches. Much more therapeutic than heavy bass blasting in the eardrums.

Time drifted. He allowed his mind to float, in an effort to blank out the conversation earlier that day. Not easy, given its magnitude, its ramifications. Still, he pushed it away, concentrated on running, putting one foot in front of the other. Mindfulness in motion.

He made his way down a long sweeping hill, reaching a section of the road hidden by high hedgerow and overarching rowan trees. The sun, momentarily, was blocked, filtered to shards of light through the leaves. He turned his head at a slight angle. Behind him, a noise. The rumbling of an engine. Powerful. Coming at speed. He looked back, swivelling round. The trees restricted his field of vision.

Suddenly, a motorbike whipped round the bend, a hundred yards from him. Gallagher was taken by surprise, felt his heart jump. He stepped to one side. The biker passed him, a fleeting image, in leathers, a black helmet and shaded visor. Gallagher shook his head. *Fucking idiot.* He resumed his run, then slowed to a walk – the biker had stopped, a hundred yards in front, where the trees thinned to more fields, still gunning the engine.

Gallagher picked up his speed, veering to the opposite side of the road. The events which followed were swift and devastating.

The biker dismounted. Gallagher was adjacent to him. The biker held a pistol, complete with silencer, took a step towards him, spaced his legs, raised his arms, aimed the weapon with a two-handed grip, fired three times. Three soft coughs. The action was executed with expertise, and lasted no longer than four seconds.

The first took Gallagher in the centre of the throat. His neck bloomed open, split down the middle, a sudden tangle of blood and vein. The impact rocked him back, but he didn't fall. He staggered on, mind not yet accepting the situation.

The second took him on the chest, piercing the sternum, eviscerating the aortic valve. This stopped him. His legs folded. He collapsed to his knees, his Nike top a vivid new colour.

The third killed him. Instant, the bullet entering his forehead creating a neat hole, exiting through the back of the skull, taking half the brain with it.

Gallagher toppled to the ground. The biker looked down, face blanked by the visor. Whether any emotion was displayed was impossible to say. A step forward. Another shot, into the head. Gallagher's face imploded, eyes, nose, mouth vanished.

The biker remained motionless for all of three seconds, then removed the silencer, tucked it and the pistol into an inside pocket, then climbed on the motorbike, and sped off.

3

Soldier, Ask Not

Desmond Gallagher was buried in a small cemetery called the Gateway Lodge, on the outskirts of East Kilbride. Adam Black attended, chosen to lower the coffin with five others. He had known Gallagher since his late teens, both in the same law class at Edinburgh University. They'd graduated, then gone separate ways.

Gallagher stayed with the law. Black joined the parachute regiment. Opposite ends of the spectrum, mused Black, as he gripped the yellow strap, and took the strain, lowering the coffin down gently. And yet they'd stayed in touch. They were friends, and had stayed friends.

When Black returned to the world of law, they got close again. He and Black had met for lunch only five weeks earlier. Black thought back. They'd chatted, shared a bottle of red. Reminisced. The talk was casual. And yet... He pondered – there was an undercurrent. A nervous edge to Gallagher's demeanour. An unease which Black couldn't quite put his finger on.

And within days, on a still summer's evening, Desmond Gallagher was murdered on a country road a mile from his house. Shot. Left to rot. Black, like everyone, like the nation, was stunned. This was an exceptional act of violence, requiring skill and foresight. Execution style. A random act? Hardly.

The gathering was large. Desmond Gallagher had been loved. He'd left a wife – Deborah – and two kids. One of them not quite a kid, reflected Black. The older one was nineteen. His younger brother was either eleven or twelve. Black couldn't recall. They stood, Desmond Gallagher's little family, garbed in black, quiet and solemn, faces pale and pinched in the bright afternoon.

For the briefest moment, Black felt a little envious. Should he die, who would mourn for him? His family were dead, he had few friends. No close relatives. He had chosen a solitary life. Enforced, perhaps. The equation was simple. If he got too close to someone, then the ending was seldom good. Death was never far away from Adam Black. It always hovered close, ready to dispense.

The priest uttered some final words. People headed back to their cars. Black made his way to Deborah, to pay final respects. She stood by her husband's graveside, skin white as marble, her children by her.

"I'm sorry, Deborah," Black said. "If there's anything I can do..."

She looked up at him, eyes round and glistening.

"You're not coming back...?"

"I wasn't..."

"Please," she urged. "Come back to the house. A last farewell. He would have wanted that."

"Of course."

She touched his elbow with her fingers, hesitated.

"There's something..."

"Yes?"

"There's something I want to show you."

4

The drive back to Desmond Gallagher's house took only fifteen minutes. Black was part of a procession of vehicles. Friends, relatives, heading back for food and drinks – *a last farewell*. Black had never been to Thorntonhall. He'd been asked back many times, for dinner, for drinks. He'd always declined. Why? Black had no family. To mingle with another would only bring melancholy. Better rather to avoid completely.

He was mildly impressed. Houses set back some distance from a single narrow road, half hidden by trees, elegant and grand. Built on high ground, the view also was impressive – green fields and woodland, and in the distance, the sprawling mass of Glasgow, beyond which, clear in the afternoon sun, the sweep of hills and trees.

Not a bad place to live, thought Black. If you could afford it. Which few could. But Desmond Gallagher had done well, and it was no secret. One of the top human rights lawyers in the country, he deserved to live in a place like this. Black reflected. Perhaps. But he didn't deserve to be murdered.

He arrived at the house, and parked on the pavement outside. The place was already full of cars. A house built fifty yards back, quaint with its white brick walls and black trimmed windows and crow-stepped gables. Hanging baskets emblazoned the entrance with colour. Cradled in the low branches of an ancient tree, a tree house with a rope ladder. On one side, a large conservatory, and as Black approached, he saw it was busy with people.

Black entered. He was met by one of the sons. The younger boy. Tony. He nodded at Black solemnly, his face stern and intense. He didn't know who Black was. He spoke with rigid formality. A seriousness way beyond his years. "If you'd like to make your way through, please."

"Thank you."

Black made his way to the kitchen. In the centre island, caterers had laid out trays of cold food and paper plates and plastic cutlery. Also bottles of wine and soft drinks, and rows of glasses. Black poured himself a glass of red. People stood in small clusters, talking quietly. He went through to the conservatory. Some he recognised – other lawyers. Most he didn't know. He smiled, and stood to one side, gazing at the back garden. It was neat and simple. Lawn, flowers on either side, a back wall, beyond which, woodland. The conservatory doors were open, leading to a wide decking. There, chairs and recliners, a couple of patio heaters, and a barrel-style barbeque. Black imagined Gallagher here, with his family, and friends, flipping burgers, drinking beer, talking politics.

Politics. Black thought back. Gallagher was involved heavily in human rights and Immigration Law. A million miles from criminal and civil work, conveyancing, chamber practice. The usual stuff which made most lawyers tick. Human rights however – to Black, to master such a thing, a person had to be half politician, half activist, half lawyer. Too many halves for Black. But Gallagher was all of those, and more. Gallagher cared for his fellow man. Perhaps, Black mused, the essence of a true lawyer. Upholder of the law, defender of the weak.

His thoughts were interrupted. A young man approached. Gallagher's older son. Fresh-faced, hair shaved to the bone above the ears, a skim of bristle at the top, his expression clear and candid. He looked strong and capable. His suit masked a lean muscularity. He moved with an easy, almost languid competence.

"Captain Black?"

Black nodded, somewhat bemused. "I haven't been called Captain for a while."

The young man put his hand out. "I'm Chris Gallagher. I'm glad you came, sir."

Black nodded, gave a small sad smile, shook his hand. "I'm deeply sorry, Chris. I knew your dad from way back. You and I have met before, when you were much younger. You might not remember."

Chris Gallagher's face displayed no reaction. "Bad time," he said simply. "My father spoke highly of you. He told me you'd joined the army after you got your degree."

"I did the stint at Sandhurst. Officer training. Then straight into the parachute regiment. A million miles from a law office. And if I remember, you enlisted last year?"

Chris smiled, showing white teeth. "Parachute Regiment. 2nd Battalion. Based at Colchester Barracks. Joined at seventeen."

"Your father was proud of you."

Chris's bottom lip trembled. Black knew he was holding back.

"How many jumps you made?"

Chris's face brightened. "Lost count."

Black put his hand on his shoulder, gripped it firmly. "That's the answer."

Chris hesitated, then spoke. "You were a Captain in the SAS?"

"For my sins."

"My father told me you won a medal."

"A very long time ago. The stuff of ancient history."

Chris's eyes shone with tears. "It's such an honour to talk to you." His voice broke. "We don't deserve it."

Black regarded him curiously. "Deserve?"

Suddenly, the young man leant forward, embraced Black, and held him close.

"Thank you for coming," he whispered. Black detected the unmistakable smell of whisky. Chris stepped back, gave a tremulous smile, made his way out of the conservatory and into the back garden, to stand to one side, a lonely and forlorn figure.

The boy was grief-stricken. Maybe even a little in shock. Black wondered – how would he react, if his father had been murdered? It was idle to speculate. Each man deals with death in his own way. Except the whisky, usually the common denominator. Whisky oiled the machine, smoothed out the bumps, made the whole crazy thing easier to endure.

He knew the answer to the question – if his own father had been murdered, shot in the road and left to die, Black would have craved oblivion. No doubt about it. Lose himself in several bottles of booze. And afterwards? Black knew the answer to that as well.

Questions would be asked. Blood would spill.

But this wasn't his fight. Not today. He sipped his wine, preferring his own company, and let the people round him talk.

5

The guests filtered out, gradually, each offering quiet condolences to Deborah as they left. Chris, her son, stood with her. Tony was nowhere to be seen. It was 5pm. The sky was overcast, the sun hidden behind straggles of grey cloud. Looked like it might rain, thought Black. The last guest had left. All the food had been consumed. The wine too.

Deborah gave a weak smile, and went over to Black, standing in a corner of the conservatory. "Thanks for coming." She touched his hand with the tip of her finger. "Would you like something stronger? I know I would. Desmond said you were fond of Glenfiddich."

"He knew me," said Black. "That would be nice."

Deborah Gallagher was an attractive woman. Early forties, dark curls and olive pale skin. Medium height. Dark hazel eyes. Slim. She kept herself in shape. They'd first met years ago, when she was Desmond Gallagher's girlfriend, before they got married. Black reached back. How long ago? Maybe twenty years, he reckoned. Maybe twenty-five. The thought suddenly depressed him. So much had happened. His wife and child murdered. Now Deborah's husband murdered. A cruel symmetry.

She pulled out a bottle from a kitchen cupboard. Fifteen-year-old Glenfiddich. She poured it into two crystal glasses. "Neat?"

"It's the only proper way to enjoy a single malt. In my opinion."

She handed a glass to Black.

"To Desmond," she said quietly. She raised her glass.

Black did the same, sipped the whisky. It tasted good.

Black waited. He wasn't entirely sure what to say. Words at this time felt hollow. Sometimes silence was best. Eventually he spoke.

"How are the kids bearing up? I met Chris. A fine young man. I think he'll do well."

She heaved a deep shuddering sigh. Black admired her self-containment.

"Chris, I think... he still can't believe it. It's shaken him. But he puts on such a brave front. They teach that, don't they, Adam? In the army. Stiff upper lip."

"Soldiers are human beings. We bleed, we cry, like anyone else."

"Tony's taken it badly. He barely leaves his room. When he does, he doesn't talk. He keeps everything inside. He's such a sweet child. Sensitive. Always has been. Twelve years old, and this shit happens. I wonder if he'll ever get over it."

Black responded, his voice soft. "He will. I have no doubt. He's young, and he has time on his side. To heal. The human body – the mind – can repair. With a little help. You'll all need help, I think, to get over this. But you will, I promise."

She looked up at him suddenly, eyes brimming with tears. "You promise? Did you repair, Adam? When your family was murdered?"

Black sad nothing. Hollow words. Yet he had meant what he'd said.

"I'm sorry, Adam. I shouldn't have said that. That was just crass."

"Not at all. It's a difficult, terrible, impossible time."

She gave a small tight smile. She was trying hard not to cry. She bit her bottom lip, blinked away tears. "Come with me," she said. "I want to show you something."

He followed her, out of the kitchen, to the hallway, and upstairs to the first floor, and then to a door at the end of a corridor. She turned. "His study."

They entered. It was a room of regular dimensions. A solid oak desk and on it, a computer screen and a keyboard. A silver-plated pen holder. Some office gadgets: pendulum balls; a revolving orbit. Also, a framed photograph of Desmond Gallagher and his family, sitting round a dining table. Gallagher was showing a beaming smile for the camera, as was Deborah. The two boys, Black noted, were reserved, faces straight and serious.

Files were stacked on one side. Shelves lined a wall, with more files. And books. Lots of books, arranged neatly in rows. All legal. The desk faced a large window, offering a clear and stunning vista. Black pictured Gallagher working here, looking up from his files, gazing outside – the distant hills, and on a clear crisp afternoon, snow-topped mountains far away.

"When he wasn't in his office, he was here," said Deborah, more to herself than Black. "He was never far from his work. The police have taken everything. His files. His computer, his hard drive. Except for this."

She pulled out a drawer of the desk, and took out a file, which she placed on the smooth oak surface. A heading sheet had been stapled to the front cover. On it, typed, were two words: **Remus Syndicate.**

"Have you heard of this?" asked Deborah.

Black shook his head.

"Take a look."

Black picked up the file. Inside, treasury tagged, were two envelopes.

"Open them," said Deborah.

Black opened the first. Inside, folded, an A4 sheet of paper, which he carefully pulled out. Typewritten, were the following words: *Let Remus go. First warning.*

Black raised an eyebrow. He turned his attention to the second envelope, repeated the process.

You were warned. Time to die.

Black looked at Deborah, bemused.

"What *is* this?"

"These were sent to us. The date stamp on the first is eight weeks ago. The second, two days before Desmond was murdered. I found them in this file, in his drawer."

"You showed them to the police?"

"Of course. But they've come up blank. So they say."

"So they say?"

"The truth? I don't trust anyone. Desmond was working on something huge. The biggest case of his life. His words. And he was scared. He told me it was something terrible. That he'd uncovered something monstrous. Again, his words. But he couldn't tell anyone, because he didn't know who to tell, because no one could be trusted. Terrible crimes were being committed. And the people involved were powerful."

"Did he say who?"

"No. He rarely spoke about his work. But this was different. This... shook him. All I've got is the heading on the file."

"The Remus Syndicate."

She nodded.

Black took a deep breath. "This is a police matter, Deborah.

If whoever sent these letters had something to do with Desmond's death, then the police are the best people to deal with it. Let them do their job."

She responded, her voice brittle. "He didn't trust the police. I'm scared, Adam. I'm scared for my children. If these people can kill Desmond, then what's to stop them from coming after us. You understand? It would be logical – they might assume Desmond told me something. What then?"

"There's nothing to be done. Your husband was murdered. An awful crime was committed. We have a justice system."

She glared at him. "Fuck the justice system! Tell me, Adam, what did you do, when your wife and daughter were murdered!"

Black had no answer to give. She of course had no real idea what he'd done in the aftermath of their deaths – that he'd hunted down the killers and extinguished their existence without compunction. But he understood. He understood the raw rage, the inadequacy, the craving for revenge.

He understood.

"Will you help us?" she said, voice a dull monotone. "If there's anyone in this world who can find who did this... fucking obscenity, it's you! You're trained. You know these people. You know how they act. You're..."

"...one of them?"

She sank into the chair at the desk, buried her face in her hands, shed soft tears. "I'm sorry. I'm drowning and I'm scared. Please forgive me."

"There's nothing to forgive. Desmond worked with one partner, yes?"

She looked up, rubbed away tears. "Yes?"

"What's his name?"

"Charley. Charley Sinclair. He was here briefly. I should have introduced him. But he was gone before I got the chance. Why?"

Black had made his decision. Deborah was right. He was

trained. Trained in dealing in death, and all that came with it. She had asked for his help, because she knew he could. Was he just the same as those who had murdered her husband? The answer was an unequivocal yes. Set a killer to catch a killer.

And for a man like Black, killing was easy, because he was so damned good at it.

"Charley Sinclair. I'll pay him a visit."

6

People sleep peaceably in their beds at night only because rough men stand ready to do violence on their behalf.
— George Orwell

Black decided to visit the lawyer called Charley Sinclair the following day. It was a Saturday. Black didn't think Sinclair would be working, and went to his home address, provided by Deborah. He lived in a town twenty miles from Glasgow, called Strathaven. A place built round a common green, with a sprinkling of craft shops and coffee houses and small bohemian-style restaurants. A straggling stream twisted like a grey vein through its centre, straddled by an ancient humpbacked bridge. Near the centre, the ruins of Strathaven Castle, comprising little more than a turret and some derelict walls.

Black knew little of the town, nor did he want to, particularly. He found Sinclair's house easily enough. A sprawling new build, on a characterless estate set on the periphery. It was 9.30am. He parked his car on the road adjacent.

The sky was overcast, a tinge of rain in the air. Dark clouds loomed. In the driveway, a 4x4 sapphire-black Jaguar.

Black made his way to the front door – a rather ostentatious pillared entrance. He rang the doorbell. The glass was bevelled, imbued with a floral design. He detected movement inside. A man answered, opening the door just wide enough for his face to peer through.

"Yes?"

Black regarded him. Pale skin stretched taut over the angular bones of his face; wispy brown hair styled back from a receding forehead. He seemed in a state of nervous emotion. His eyes darted to Black, and beyond, then back to Black.

"Charley Sinclair?"

Sinclair compressed his lips, blinked. "Who sent you?"

Black gave a humourless smile. "Interesting way to answer the door."

"It's a simple question."

"I haven't been sent. I was a friend of Desmond's. My name's Adam Black. I want to talk. About Desmond."

Sinclair seemed to consider, his forehead wrinkling in a frown. "Adam Black... Desmond talked about you. The soldier. You were at his funeral."

"Yes."

It was Sinclair's turn to smile. Like Black's, there was little humour in it.

"You're on your own?"

"Only me."

"Then you can come in."

Odd, thought Black. He entered.

He was led through a spacious hallway, and into a kitchen at the rear. It was large, gleaming with cream tiles. A double range oven, massive American fridge freezer, the doors of which spotted with a colourful display of fridge magnets. A breakfast bar of solid grey granite along one end, lined with high stools. Beyond, wide patio doors, opening to a decked area shaded by a bright red awning, stepping onto a neat garden.

The place was uncluttered. On the worktop, a bowl of fruit. Beside it, a bottle of gin, half empty, a bottle of tonic water, and a crystal glass. Black watched, as Sinclair poured a healthy measure of gin, a splash of tonic, and drank it in two gulps. His hands were trembling. He repeated the process, pouring in gin, some tonic.

"Can I tempt you?"

"It's a tad early," Black said.

"Fuck it. You're out of bed, aren't you?"

Sinclair opened a cupboard, got another glass, poured some for Black, and slid it across the surface.

"If you don't want it, fine. It won't go to waste."

Black said nothing.

Sinclair took another drink, closed his eyes as the alcohol slid down his throat.

"I should have spoken to you at the funeral," he said at length. "Fucking bad business."

"Shot and left for dead," replied Black. "Clinical. Perhaps you're right."

"Right about what?"

"A bad business. Because to me, that's how it looks. His death was almost businesslike. Someone knew where he'd be. The spot was well chosen. The kill was... efficient. As I said, businesslike."

Sinclair took a deep shuddering breath, slung back another mouthful of gin. His voice was tainted with the slightest slur.

"How did you know him?"

"We went to university together. Same law class."

"But divergent paths, I think. He talked about you a lot. He told me you joined the army."

Black nodded.

"Adam Black..." Sinclair took another slug. "SAS. Yes?"

Black nodded.

"You guys. Real hard nuts. Killers. You a killer, Adam?"

He stared at Black, with round glassy eyes. The drink was taking its toll.

Black essayed a sympathetic smile. "How are you bearing up?"

"Bearing up? My partner's been shot. I've still got a law practice to run." He poured another inch of gin, dispensed with the tonic, drank it straight. His lips puckered as he downed the liquid.

Keep going, Black thought. The more he consumed, the more garrulous he would become.

"Will you cope?" ventured Black. "On your own? I dare say Desmond left a big space."

Sinclair gave a sour laugh. "You never answered my question."

Black said nothing.

"Desmond said you won a medal. Said you're a fucking hero."

"I'm no hero. Tell me about Desmond. Human rights lawyer. That's a pretty niche area of law. You worked on cases together?"

Sinclair's gaze drifted, as if he was recollecting. Eventually he spoke, his voice a low mutter.

"The whole thing's fucked."

"Tell me," said Black softly.

Sinclair blinked. His eyes suddenly glistened with tears.

"You ever crossed the line? Ever journeyed down the dark path?"

"Have you?"

"It's complicated."

"It always is. Did the Remus Syndicate make it complicated, Charley?"

Sinclair spoke as if he hadn't heard. "Are you a killer, Adam?"

The doorbell chimed. Sinclair finished his drink. The bottle was almost empty. He lifted it to his lips, and drained the contents.

Black waited.

The bell chimed again.

Sinclair gripped the edge of the breakfast bar, steadying himself. "I need to get that."

Whoever was outside was rapping the door hard.

"Someone's keen to see you," said Black.

"Very keen," mumbled Sinclair. He snapped his head up, gave Black a wild look.

"I didn't ask you to come. You can still get out. Through the back garden. They'll never see you."

"Why would I do that, Charley?"

"I don't know what they'll do. They're... monsters."

The knocking got louder, the door rattling, the sound echoing through the house.

"Who's out there?" Black asked, a whisper of dread in his chest.

"Run, Adam," Sinclair rasped. "Run!"

7

Haytham Bustan sat in a coffee shop on Victoria Road. He owned the establishment. Or more particularly, he owned the company which owned the establishment. Bustan didn't want his name linked directly with anything. Laundering money was a complex business.

Bustan was a complex man. He had, over the years, sprinkled money in many diverse areas. Property and land. The stock market. Various businesses. He owned a taxi company, and five car washes. Plus a chain of nail bars and tanning salons. A wide-ranging portfolio. His name was hidden, beneath layers of documentation. Confuse, complicate, befuddle. By the time the authorities caught up, if they ever did, he would be long gone. Back to Turkey, to live like a prince.

Everything emanated from hard cash. The amount he got for the refugees was, even by his own standards, extravagant. It was a Saturday morning, and Bustan sat in his coffee shop, waiting for the cash deposit. Six weeks earlier, he had delivered six people. Six *bodies.* Which meant, in his estimation, £240,000. They never failed to pay. Every six weeks. Punctual and reliable.

He sat, sipping a double-shot espresso, and wished to fuck he'd got into this business years ago.

The coffee shop was unspectacular. Blink and you'd miss it. Which was the idea. Nothing showy or ostentatious. The opposite. The exterior was drab. Wooden cladding painted pale green, peeling and stained. Inside was gloomy. The floor was black tiled linoleum, laid a hundred years ago. The walls yellowy white, with framed pictures on the wall, of nameless faces and places. A single glass counter, exhibiting rows of unappealing rolls and sandwiches, and behind the counter, a fat man sat on a stool. The fat man was an old friend of Bustan's, born in the same shithole part of Istanbul. His name was Yousef Kaya. Yousef Kaya killed people, and enjoyed doing it. Which was why Bustan found him useful.

Bustan sat in a corner, at a table upon which was a single cup and saucer. Four others sat hunched round an adjacent table, playing cards, drinking strong coffee. Cousins. All part of the organisation. Friends and family. Bustan reflected – he'd heard the old adage a thousand times. *Friends and business, oil and water.* Incompatible. Bustan however regarded the notion as bullshit. Blood you could trust. Friendships going back to the shared experience of dirt and poverty and violence could be counted on.

Every man in that room would die for Bustan. Their loyalty was beyond money. Was beyond question. Bustan sipped his coffee. Would he die for any of these men? Hardly. It was a one-way arrangement.

Apart from Bustan and his men, the place was empty. It was always empty. It was 10am. Exactly on time, two men entered. Well dressed. Wearing tight-cut sombre blue suits, crisp white shirts, dark ties. Both sporting crew cuts. Clean shaven. Muscular. Ex-military, probably, thought Bustan. The Syndicate would employ the best. But in the dirt and grime of a street fight, when knives were out, and blood was high, he wondered how such men would fare.

One carried a small metal briefcase. They spotted him immediately, nodded, made their way over. The four other men playing cards stopped their chatting, stared like hyenas. The fat man eased off his chair, locked the door.

"Welcome." Bustan gestured to the chairs on the opposite side of his table. The men didn't offer any pleasantries. The one with the briefcase sat, set the briefcase on the table. The other hovered three paces back, watchful.

"Your friend is always so anxious-looking," said Bustan, the edges of his mouth curling into a smile. "Tell him to sit. Relax. Coffee? Yousef makes it strong and good. Turkish. The way it should be made. Yes, Yousef?"

The fat man – Yousef Kaya – had remained at the door. He had flipped the "open" to "closed". He stared back with round button-black eyes.

Bustan shrugged. "Yousef doesn't speak much English." He gave a humourless chuckle. "He prefers kofta to talking."

The man opposite remained expressionless. "No coffee, thanks." He opened the briefcase, swivelled it round to face Bustan. It was packed neatly with £50 notes. He reached into his pocket, produced a mobile phone, placed it on the table beside the briefcase, pressed the keypad. A voice spoke. It was harsh, metallic. Disguised through a voice modulator.

"The goods were spoiled."

Bustan licked his lips. Not what he was expecting. He saw the look on his cousins' faces, their demeanour change. Unlike Yousef, they spoke good English.

Bustan maintained his easy smile. "What has this got to do with me? This is not my concern. I gave you six. I get paid for six.

The arithmetic is easy, yes?" He gave another rumbling laugh, took another sip.

"You brought six to the table," replied the voice. "But I repeat. Two were spoiled."

Bustan ran a hand through his wispy dark hair. "Spoiled? Sorry, am I missing something?"

"The man and woman. They were riddled with cancer. Had to be written off. We don't pay for write-offs."

"Meaning?"

"Meaning we're not paying for ruined meat. There's £160,000 in the case. Next time, make sure the merchandise is clean."

Bustan leaned back in his chair, gazing at the man sitting opposite. His face betrayed no emotion. It was like looking at carved wood.

"Next time? Maybe there won't be a next time."

"You think you're special, Bustan?" replied the voice. "There's a queue of greedy fuckers like you. If you're not happy, that's fine. Take the money, and it ends. Let's see how long you and your puny band of jumped-up gangsters last without the cash."

Bustan took a deep breath, spoke as if the voice of reason. "How can I know if they have cancer. Or Liver disease. Or Hepatitis. Or the fucking clap, for that matter. I bring them. You do what you do with them."

"It's bad luck, Bustan. But we're not paying for stuff we can't use."

Bustan shifted in his chair. His cousins watched him. The two men were undoubtedly carrying weapons. Plus they would have backup.

Almost as if the voice on the phone could read his thoughts, it spoke again.

"If you're thinking of a little bloodshed, then there are two cars outside. Ten men. If you want to display some of that hot

Turkish temper, then we come down on you like a fucking whirlwind. That shithole you're in will be the last thing you'll see, and you can wave goodbye to your fucking castle in Istanbul. Take the money, Bustan. Move on."

One of the cousins got to his feet, went over to the window, peered out. He turned, nodded at Bustan.

This situation was unexpected. Bustan was caught. He could either start a war he could not possibly win, or accept the insult to his pride and self-esteem. Fuck pride. Bustan didn't want to die.

He closed the briefcase, and placed it on the floor by his feet.

The man sitting opposite him grunted. "Good choice."

Bustan resumed his smile, finished his coffee. Back to business. "We have another batch coming in Tuesday evening. Another family."

"How many?" replied the voice.

"Two adults, three children."

Silence. Then the voice spoke again, deep and brassy. "This is from the top. Change of plan."

Bustan raised an eyebrow. "What change?"

"We don't want the adults. Only the kids."

Bustan asked the question, but he thought he already knew the answer. "Why?"

"You know why. They're cleaner."

"And what will I do with their parents?"

Laughter, sounding like the turn of rusty wheels. "Do what you do best, Bustan."

The line went dead. The man picked up the phone, put it back in his pocket. He stood, acknowledged Bustan with the briefest of nods, and he and his associate made their way out. Yousef Kaya rattled the bolt, opened the main door. They left. Bustan watched them go.

Do what you do best.

Three children. £40,000 each. £120,000 total. He would kill his own mother for that type of money.

The parents would not present a problem to Haytham Bustan.

8

Black had no intention of running. "What's going on, Charley?" he said softly.

Charley didn't respond. He closed his eyes, rubbed them with his fingers, opened them. They were dull, resigned. The banging at the front door was relentless.

"They're not going to go," said Black.

"I know." Charley stared at Black, pressed the back of his hand to his mouth. He began to sob. "They're going to kill me."

Black said nothing.

"Will you help me, Adam?"

"Why don't you answer the door before they break it down."

"Yes," mumbled Sinclair. "Before they break it down. Fuck them."

He swayed slightly, made his way from the kitchen, back through the hall. Black waited. He heard the door being unlocked, then voices. The door closing. Footsteps approaching. Black moved swiftly, went over to the kitchen units, opened drawers. There! A tray of knives. He picked one out – a six-inch filleting knife. A sharp little fucker. He placed it in the back pocket of his jeans. Black had no idea what he was to confront. He stood, senses heightened to an increased competence.

Sinclair entered. He was followed by two men. The first was about five ten, shorter than Black by a clear four inches, but thick in the neck and shoulders, wide at the hip: attributes indicating strength and agility. His head was small, shaved to the bone. Flat nose, dark eyes. He had a calm air, lips curled in a secret half-smile.

The other was taller, slim, long-legged. Muscular shoulders. Dancing slate-grey eyes. Unlike his friend, his hair was long, black as a raven, coiffured back from his forehead, and over his ears. Neat compact features. He seemed charged with a nervous vitality. Both looked eminently capable. And highly dangerous.

Sinclair made his way back over to the breakfast bar. The two men stopped when they saw Black. They stood, maybe seven feet from him.

"You didn't say you had a guest," said the smaller one. He spoke with an accent. North of England, guessed Black, Yorkshire, maybe. "Aren't you going to introduce us?"

Sinclair's voice was heavy and slurred. He was half-pissed.

"Adam Black. Meet fucking Laurel and Hardy."

The smile never left the smaller man's face. "Charley's not being very polite." His tone was soft, sardonic. "I think maybe he's had a little too much to drink. You're Adam Black? My name's Daniel. My good friend here is Tristan. It's a pleasure to meet you, Adam Black."

"The pleasure's all mine. No second names?" Black shrugged. "I think I prefer Laurel and Hardy."

The man with the dancing eyes – Tristan – took a sharp intake of breath, stepped forward, to be halted by Daniel's raised arm.

"Mr Black's only joshing. You're a funny man. But fun time's over. We have important things to discuss with Charley. Private matters. I'm sure you understand." Daniel gestured to the kitchen door. "So, if you wouldn't mind. Perhaps you and Charley can catch up another time."

Black's expression changed to surprise. "But you're the reason I'm here, gentlemen. Charley asked me to come. To speak for him, as it were. As his lawyer."

"What the fuck!" exclaimed Tristan.

Daniel merely laughed. "Two lawyers in the one room. Talk about bad luck. I think a mistake's been made. Charley doesn't need a lawyer." Daniel swivelled his head. "You don't need a lawyer, do you, Charley?"

Sinclair didn't respond immediately. His face was slack, devoid of animation. He muttered something. "I'm sorry."

Daniel clapped his hands. "There we are. He's sorry. Sorry for wasting your time. Now, Mr Black, if you'll excuse us."

Black turned to a kettle on the kitchen top next to him, switched it on.

"What are you doing?" Daniel asked softly.

"Getting a coffee. I think it's going to be a long morning."

"Are you a fucking stand-up comedian!" Tristan's face had reddened, eyes darting from the kettle to Black like fireflies.

"Easy," soothed Daniel. His mouth curled into a sad droop. "Mr Black doesn't fully understand the nature of the situation." His gave Black a fixed stare, as if trying to derive meaning from Black's actions. "I won't ask again."

Black reacted by leaning back against a kitchen cupboard, and folding his arms. He gave a wintry grin.

"Seeing as you're asking, I'll answer that in the negative. I think I'll stay, thank you."

He appraised the two men. Both in apparent good condition, at the peak of their physical prowess. But then so was Black. The man calling himself Daniel seemed disciplined, measured. Tristan on the other hand, seemed reckless. But still a handful.

"Let's make this easy," Daniel said. "Let's ask Charley what he wants. After all, he's your client."

He turned his attention to Sinclair, who stared back, his expression one of dreamy confusion.

"Tell Mr Black you would like him to leave."

Sinclair puckered his lips, wrinkled his nose, as if giving the question deep thought. "Did I tell you that Adam Black was in the SAS." He waved his arm vaguely. "He's a fucking killing machine. That's why he's here."

He had both Tristan and Daniel's full attention.

"And why exactly *is* he here?" said Daniel.

"To kill you. Why else?"

"Really? How interesting."

Black regarded Sinclair with a burning gaze. He felt like throttling him. Matters had just got a million times worse.

Daniel scrutinised Black with renewed intensity. "SAS? We're shaking in our boots."

"Best you go your way," Black replied in a mild voice. "I am a dangerous man."

He straightened, arms loose and easy at his side. In such situations, when danger was close, Black possessed the ability to detach his mind, and watch almost as a spectator, brushing aside fear and doubt. It was thus he watched the two men before him.

Daniel glanced at Sinclair. "This will not go well for you, Charley."

He turned back to Black, stepped to one side, showed his sad twisted smile, gave a delicate shrug, from which Tristan seemed to derive exact information. In his hand was a blade. A hunting knife. He strode forward. The kettle clicked. Black reached over, grabbed it, flung the boiling water into Tristan's face. Tristan recoiled, shrieking. The knife fell with a clatter.

Daniel moved, darted forward with deceiving speed, and

with agility, swung up his leg, designed to cripple, or even kill. Black dodged, seized the heel and toe of his shoe, twisted, intending to break the ankle. Daniel turned in mid-air, pulled himself in a ball, wrenched his foot from Black's grasp, landed with a roll on the kitchen floor, and like a cat, bounced to his feet.

Black didn't stop. He had the momentum. He had the kitchen knife in his hand, crouched, thrust his arm forward, a quick, savage movement, stabbed Tristan in the thigh. Tristan instinctively doubled over. Black caught the back of his head, yanked Tristan's face against his upraised knee, crushing bone, breaking teeth. Tristan staggered, fell on his backside, dazed. Blood oozed from his leg, and both nostrils. Broken nose, possibly broken jaw.

Daniel took a deep breath, regarding Black with a new respect. Tristan moaned. Blood leaked from his leg onto the kitchen tiles at an alarming rate.

"Looks like your pal is dying," said Black, ignoring the sprawled figure of Tristan, concentrating entirely on Daniel. The easy smile had left Daniel's face. Now, a mixture of anger and confusion.

"Pick him up and get the hell out of here," continued Black in a flat, hard voice. "I won't ask again."

Daniel inclined his head. "Touché."

He bent, heaved Tristan up. Tristan tried to speak, managing an inarticulate mumble. He hooked his arm round Daniel's shoulders, leant heavily on him. Daniel clasped Tristan's waist, manoeuvred his way out of the kitchen. Daniel turned as he was leaving.

"I'll look forward to meeting you soon, Mr Black."

"It will be my pleasure."

Without further comment, Tristan and Daniel left the house.

Black filled the kettle up with water, switched it on, fixed his attention on Sinclair. Sinclair stared at him, blinked.

"Jesus fucking Christ," he slurred. "You're making a coffee, after… all that. You're one cool-headed bastard."

"The coffee's for you, Charley," Black snapped. "Time to sober up. Time to tell me what the fuck you've done."

9

Rosewood Hospital was set in several hundred acres of carefully managed woodland, six miles from Troon. It was a place not easily found, reached by back roads and single lanes. Private, secluded. Treatment only for those wealthy enough to afford it. One hundred beds. Each room with en suite facilities, satellite TV, and telephone. Ten consultancy rooms. Ten operating theatres. Fifteen full-time consultants. Able to accommodate everything – from hip replacement to bowel cancer.

The promise? A patient could be on the operating table within forty-eight hours of diagnosis. Such service came at a price. Initial consultation would never be less than £2,000. Then it was a rocket to the moon, depending on the ailment, and the seriousness. Anything from £10,000 to £100,000. And beyond. They took referrals from doctors, hospitals, and self-referrals. They took everything. Nothing was too small, or too big. Each of the consultants was easily a millionaire. Money, money, money.

Michael Stapleton was head consultant, and a surgeon with over thirty-five years' experience. Which meant, essentially, he was in charge. Also, he was CEO of the private limited company governing the hospital. As such, in his particular world, he was a powerful man.

The hospital was modern, a cuboid of glass, steel and white concrete. Four floors, plus a basement. All straight lines and clean angles. Stapleton sat in a room on the fourth floor. The conference room. Dominated by a large circular table cleverly constructed of bronze and wood. Around it, sixteen chairs.

The walls were smooth and crisp white, devoid of ornamentation, save a single painting – a swirl of vibrant colour, with no discernible shape or pattern. Entitled *Chaos*. An example, apparently, of contemporary art. More specifically, abstract expressionism. By an unknown German painter. Stapleton had bought it as an investment. He hated it. He hated it, because he didn't understand it. In Stapleton's world, things had to compute. He stared at it, as he always did, when he was in this room, trying to derive meaning, but finding none.

On the table were two bottles of mineral water. One sparkling, one still. Four glasses. Plus a silver container of coffee, and four cups, milk and sugar.

Sitting to his left was Jason Drummond. Head of security. He was sipping some water. A slab-sided face, close-cropped white hair, a short neck as wide as his head. Stocky and muscular. Stapleton, for a second, studied the thick hand holding the glass, as Drummond raised it to his mouth, and wondered what such a hand was capable of. Dark deeds, no doubt. Which was why Stapleton employed him.

To his left sat two men. One, a razor thin sandy-haired man with a complexion the colour of dull paste. Roger Dupont. Dupont regarded those beside him, with an inquisitive, almost bird-like scrutiny. A necessary evil, thought Stapleton. Dupont was head of finance, an accountant, and a veritable wizard with money, and where to put it. And as such, indispensable to the Syndicate.

The third man was a heart surgeon, renowned in his field. Percy Canning. Early forties, delicate features, quiet and composed. Articulate, intelligent.

Stapleton addressed his head of security, Jason Drummond. "What's your prediction?"

Drummond put the glass of water down, rested both his hands on the table, regarded Stapleton with eyes like black stones. He spoke in a flat voice, his face expressionless as a block of wood.

"Bustan is loyal only to money. He knows he gets well paid. He'll never bite the hand that feeds. Not unless the money runs dry. And the only way that will happen is if he fails to deliver. Bustan won't allow that to happen."

"No... how can I put it... repercussions?" Stapleton said.

Drummond gave his head the minutest of shakes. "No chance. We gave him less money, but still enough to get his cock hard. At worst, his pride's been dented. But now Bustan knows."

"Knows what?" It was the accountant who spoke up, the words rattling out. Roger Dupont. When he spoke, he blinked, as if his thoughts raced at the same speed as his voice. Drummond fixed his slab face towards Dupont. Two polar opposites, thought Stapleton. The mouse and the lion.

"He knows we make the rules. You've reminded him of this."

"And the next delivery?" Stapleton asked.

Drummond shook his head. "Nothing changes. Three units to be delivered on Tuesday evening, as per usual."

"Children." Percy Canning's voice was soft and lilting. "You made that clear?"

"Crystal. He'll not let us down."

Stapleton cleared his throat. "Are there any other issues? Anything worrying you?"

"Nothing. With the lawyer gone, life should resume as normal."

"Should?"

"There are no guarantees in this game. But Desmond Gallagher was a crusader. There aren't many lawyers like him. He's been removed from the equation. My gut feeling is that any interest in Remus has died with him."

Stapleton blew through his lips. "Let's hope your gut feeling proves to be correct."

"It usually is."

"Fair enough," said Stapleton. "Thank you, Mr Drummond. You've been very helpful."

Drummond got to his feet, gave a terse nod, left the room.

Stapleton turned to Roger Dupont. "Yes, Roger?" Dupont's lips twitched into the semblance of a smile. He reached to a slim grey leather attaché case at his feet, placed it on the table before him, opened it, pulled out three A4-sized sheets of paper, giving one to both Stapleton and Canning, keeping one for himself.

"The data's all there. Our Chinese partners are very pleased. The funds are in, and they're gasping for the next batch."

"Shame about the mother and father," said Stapleton. "They could have fetched us how much? Another twenty million? Pity."

"Disappointing," said Canning, running his eyes down the words and numbers on the sheet of paper. "Still, gross forty million. We ought not to complain. Not for an evening's work."

"Ten million a unit," said Dupont. "Despite the parents being a total loss, it was still a good day. Four complete 'hollow outs'. Every item in hot demand. You're right. We shouldn't complain. And if we stick to kids, then there's no reason why these figures can't continue." He fidgeted in his seat. "Perhaps we could even consider upping our prices."

Stapleton gave a cold laugh. "To use Drummond's expression – let's not bite the hand that feeds us. Thank you, Mr Dupont."

Dupont placed his A4 sheet in the attaché case, gave his nervous twitchy smile, and left the room.

Stapleton regarded Percy Canning. Fine, almost feminine features. Alert, lucent eyes.

Stapleton sat back. "You know, Percy, the picture on the wall. I look at it, and I see dysfunction. Confusion."

Canning turned, considered the painting, turned back. "That would be accurate, I suppose. It's called *Chaos*, after all."

"It's what I see when order is destroyed. When things turn to shit."

"Destroyed?"

"The lawyer. Desmond Gallagher. A Human rights advocate. People like that worry me. The type of person who rains down destruction on people like us. The type of person who can change all this..." Stapleton waved his arm about vaguely, gesturing the room, and everything beyond the room "... to that." He pointed at the painting on the wall. To *Chaos.* "From order to desolation. You understand what I'm saying?"

Canning cocked his head, looked at Stapleton, his delicate mouth curling into a reassuring smile.

"The lawyer is dead. The thorn in our side has been removed. Not that he posed any real threat. Let's not ask too many questions. Drummond isn't concerned. He does his business, we do ours. He doesn't see a problem. Therefore neither should we."

Stapleton was still looking at the picture. "You know what else I see?"

Canning said nothing.

"A reflection of my own fear."

"I think, Michael, you're being a tad melodramatic. Life is good. We're rich. What's not to like."

Stapleton sighed. "This is true. The money eases the guilt."

"Guilt? Fuck guilt. The people brought here are sub-human.

We do them a favour. And they do us a favour by increasing our bank balance. Exponentially. So I repeat. Fuck guilt, and everything that goes with it."

"You have a pragmatic approach to life. You stop me from being maudlin. By the way, did I mention I'd bought a villa in Tenerife?"

Canning nodded slowly, grinning. "Yummy. Tell me about it, Michael. Sounds wonderful."

10

Black and Sinclair sat on high stools, opposite each other across the breakfast bar. Blood had puddled on the tiled floor. Blood belonging once to the man called Tristan. Where Tristan was at that moment was anyone's guess. Probably the hospital, mused Black. Or maybe worse. He couldn't have cared less.

Sinclair sat hunched over a black coffee, the bones in his face pronounced and harsh. He ran a fretful hand through his hair. "You fucking showed them. You showed them what it was like."

Black had found a drinks cupboard, and helped himself to a whisky, which he'd poured into a coffee mug. He hadn't stinted. He swallowed it back, took a calming breath, focused. Black had seen violence, in all its exotic forms. The aftermath never got easier. Shock. The trick was to see it for what it was – a state of mind. Rationalise it, accept it, keep moving.

Two words knocked into him by the SAS. *Keep moving.* The antidote to shock and fear, eventually to become buried, somewhere. Black had many such buried treasures lurking deep in his mind. Someday, perhaps, a trapdoor would open, and they would come bursting out in full bright technicolour. A parade of horrors.

But not today.

He regarded Sinclair levelly. "Tell me what just happened."

Sinclair looked back at him, his eyes small and bloodshot, skin white as death. "I told you to run. Now they'll want payback."

"Who are *they?*"

"People to fear."

"That's not very helpful."

"I'm not trying to be helpful." Sinclair glared at Black. "I'm not trying to be anything. I didn't ask you to come. Look where it got you, sticking your fucking nose into other people's business."

"Who are these people, Charley?"

Sinclair remained silent for several seconds, as if deliberating his next words. He licked his lips with the tip of his tongue. "I need a drink."

"Stick to coffee. Talk to me."

Another pause. Then he spoke, his voice flat and dreary. *There sits a broken man*, thought Black.

"Can you help me, Adam?"

"I can try. But you need to open up."

Sinclair sipped his coffee, nodded, coming to some inward conclusion. "Have you heard of Malcolm Copeland?"

"No."

Sinclair gave a brittle smile. "You're lucky."

Black waited.

"I didn't really know who he was either. It's funny how things can grow from innocuous beginnings. I suppose like an itch in the cheek. Before you know it, it's full-blown skin cancer."

"Interesting comparison. Keep going."

"He was a client. Technically, he still is a client. Though the solicitor client-relationship has soured a little."

Black said nothing, took another swig of whisky, let Sinclair continue.

"I knew he was rich. He instructed us to purchase properties. 'Us' as in 'me'. Commercial units, buy-to-let investments. Glasgow, Edinburgh, all over. A businessman increasing his property portfolio. He funded everything himself. No borrowings. He didn't need the banks. But the money was clean. We did our anti-money laundering. All legitimate. All sourced. All bank transfers. Plus, he never quibbled over fees. I could charge what I wanted. Which I did." He looked at Black, almost accusing him. "So? What's not to like? I'm a lawyer trying to turn a buck. You'd have done the same."

"But things changed."

"Things always fucking change," muttered Sinclair. Another sip of coffee. His lips puckered. "This tastes fucking shit."

Black made no comment.

"We got to know each other. He's married to some trophy wife. Got two kids. He invited me to his fucking sandstone castle in the country. Barbecues, parties, dinner. He has a place in Portugal. Long weekends in the sun. He's like fucking Gatsby. I repeat, what's not to like?"

"But..."

"Of course there's a fucking but. There always is. The flip side to the dream."

"The nightmare."

"A fucking understatement. He asked me to do something."

"Of course he did."

Sinclair rubbed tears from his eyes. "He asked me to take cash. I mean hard fucking cash. Paper money in a fucking sports bag. £500,000. I was to bank it into the firm account, then use it to buy land. A one-off."

"Traditionally known as laundering."

"I did it. I got a ten per cent cut." Sinclair gave a sardonic snort. "Used it to build an extension to the house. My daughter uses it as a gym, when she's home." He lowered his head. "But she's never here. Not anymore." He seemed to lose focus, eyes fixed on his coffee cup.

"Money was transferred into the firm account. Did Desmond know about this?"

Sinclair lifted his head, turned to stare out through the patio doors. "Poor Desmond," he said quietly. He took a deep faltering breath, turned back to Black.

"Desmond knew nothing. The money was in, then out. Just another transaction. But the deed was done."

"Just so. You'd gone to the dark side. And as such, the door was open. Let me guess – the *one-off* didn't quite turn out like that."

Sinclair nodded grimly. "He asked me to do it again. I thought *what the fuck*. Once more. Another fifty grand in my back pocket. I told him I would do it, but after that, no more."

Black sipped the whisky, waited.

"But he wanted it again. And again. Every month, for the last six months. I said no. He said, if I didn't do it..."

"What?"

Sinclair started to sob.

"What did he threaten you with, Charley?"

Sinclair blinked, bottom lip trembling. He cleared his throat, found his voice. "He said he would have my daughter blinded with acid."

Black said nothing.

"I did it. The ten per cent stopped. It had evolved into pure extortion. Until..."

"Until what?"

"Desmond found out. By sheer fucking chance. I was lodging the cash in denominations. £25,000 instalments. Stretched over the month. I had opened separate accounts with different banks. I was ill for a couple of days. One of the fucking bank branches telephoned the office, to verify the cash. If I'd been there, I'd have given some bullshit explanation."

"But you weren't there. You were ill. I'm guessing Desmond took the call. I'm guessing Desmond was a little bemused."

Sinclair gave a weary sigh. "It all unravelled. Desmond confronted me. I..." Sinclair took a moment, swallowed. "I broke down. Told him everything. He said he was going to the police. I warned him. I told him if he did that, then there would be repercussions. Serious fucking repercussions. He said he was going to the police the next day. Nothing I could say would stop him."

"But he was stopped, wasn't he? What did you do, Charley?"

"My soul's going to burn, Adam."

"Yours wouldn't be the first. Tell me what happened."

"I made a call." He paused, took another breath. "I called Malcolm Copeland. I told him what had happened. I told him Desmond was going to the police."

Black waited.

"That evening, Desmond Gallagher was shot like a fucking dog. Now you know. I am the perpetrator of my friend's murder. What do you think of that?"

Black finished the whisky, regarded the man opposite. "And the two men today?"

"Copeland wants me to continue with our little arrangement. Business as usual. They're animals. They wanted to remind me that they still expect me to perform. They will not stop. They'll push and push, until I'm no use to them. Then they'll move on."

A fair approximation, thought Black. "You went to bed with organised crime. You entered their world."

"What can I do, Adam?"

"You go to the police."

Sinclair stared at Black, wide-eyed. "What happens then? My daughter wakes up with her fucking face burnt off."

"Where is she?"

"Aberdeen University, in halls of residence. She's twenty-one, and studying law. She knows nothing about this. My wife and I are divorced. Penny is all I have. These people. They can do anything. They'll find her, and do terrible things."

Sinclair began to cry, great racking sobs, hands cupped round his face.

"The police can offer witness protection." But Black knew that was bullshit. Cross people like Copeland, and sanctuary became an impossible dream. He knew, from bitter experience. First hand.

"But now you're in the fucking show!" Sinclair snarled suddenly. "You think a man like Copeland will let this go. What you did this morning? He's a fucking devil. Relentless. You embarrassed him. Now he'll fucking embarrass you back!"

Black stood. "Possibly. Sometimes, you have to turn things on its head. Sometimes, you have to bring it to them. I don't mind relentless. In fact, I'm quite good at it."

"What does that fucking mean!"

"I came here to help Desmond's wife. Find some answers. You've supplied them."

Sinclair also stood, wavering on his feet, clutching the breakfast bar for support. "Help me, Adam! What you did… I've never seen anything like it. You know about people like them. Please!"

Black appraised Sinclair. "You got Desmond killed. Through sheer greed. Even at the last, you betrayed him. Good luck, Charley. You're on your own."

Black made his way out of the kitchen, then turned. "And don't forget to clean the floor. Wouldn't want to slip on someone else's blood."

11

Malcolm Copeland did little exercise, despite his doctor's advice. He played some golf, waddling at best around a couple of holes before gasping to the club house. He occasionally went tenpin bowling with his wife and daughters. He played snooker. He had his own snooker room. That was the extent of it.

At just under eighteen stones, he knew he ought to do more. But he had no inclination. He liked his gin and his cigars. He liked fast food. He liked to sit on his arse in the cinema room he'd built at the back of his house, and watch movies and eat popcorn. He took pills for his heart, for his high blood pressure, for his diabetes.

He took pills for just about every fucking thing, he thought, as he sat in his study, ready to see Daniel. He had little plastic bottles in a neat line on a massive oaken desk. Like little soldiers. Eight in all. He'd forgotten what some of them were for.

Malcolm Copeland was obese. He was bald. He wore thick-lensed glasses. His skin was punctured with teenage acne, the scars of which had never gone away. He looked in the mirror, and saw one ugly bastard. But he didn't care. His God was money, and he had over fifty million squirrelled away. Plus, he was head of a well-organised crime unit, with his fat fingers in many pies. From drugs to blackmail. Extortion to murder. Power. It was all about power. And Copeland had plenty of it.

But he was irked. Things with Charley Sinclair had gone bad. As such, he needed answers. Hence the meeting with Daniel.

He got up, padded his way through to the guest room. The house was large and lavish, sitting in five acres of an immaculate garden. The halls were wide, the rooms were huge. He had converted the basement into a heated swimming pool, jacuzzi and sauna. He never used it. But his two kids liked it.

Copeland reached the guest room. High ceiling, French art on the walls, the carpet an inch thick, three large burgundy leather couches, clustered round a jade-green marble hearth. Above it, a huge painting of himself, beaming a white-toothed smile, decked in garish red tweed trousers and jacket, a waistcoat with gold buttons. In the crook of one arm, a hunting rifle. The background, distant mountains.

In a corner of the room, a gleaming ebony grand piano. In another corner, standing silent, dressed in a sombre dark suit, one of his men. At the far side, open double French doors, the glass imbued with French floral designs. Beyond that, the gardens. On garden chairs directly outside, sat two more of his men. One was smoking. Both chairs faced the interior of the guest room. At any one time, Copeland had three men in the house. All armed. All dangerous.

Sitting on one of the couches, was Daniel Pembrose. Copeland sat on a couch opposite. The furniture sagged under his weight.

On a low ivory framed coffee table between them was a box. Beside it an object the size and shape of a silver grenade. Copeland stretched over, opened the box, fished out a cigar. He picked up the silver object, flicked his finger on one edge. A flame appeared. He used it to light his cigar, cheeks puffing as he got the end glowing.

The sweet scent of tobacco permeated the air, smoke coiling through the room.

"Sorry about all this, Mr Copeland," said Daniel.

Copeland didn't answer immediately. He puffed at his cigar, licking pieces of the leaf from his lips. He leaned over, flicked it into an ashtray set in a lump of blue crystal. Then he spoke.

"I'm not entirely sure what you're sorry about. Your message was brief. Trouble at Charley Sinclair's house. Now you're here. Without Tristan, I might add. What happened, Daniel?"

Daniel shifted on the soft leather padding.

"We saw Charley this morning. Just like you wanted. Give him a warning. Business as usual, yes?"

"That was the idea. Fairly simple, I would have thought."

"Things got a little... well, fucked up."

"That's an interesting description. It conjures up a whole range of unlikely scenarios. Perhaps you'd care to elaborate? If it's not too much trouble."

Daniel cleared his throat. "We arrived. Charley was there. But he was with someone. I'd never met him before. He was... capable."

Copeland's face folded into a cold smile. "Another interesting expression."

"We told him to get the hell out. That we were there to talk to Charley. But he wasn't for budging. Said he was Charley's lawyer. But he didn't behave like any lawyer I've met."

"So we have a what... a capable lawyer? I'm still struggling to see how this reached into the realms of *fucked up*."

"The guy wasn't for leaving. You know how Tristan is. He gets a bit frenzied when things don't go his way. He went for the guy." Daniel fell silent, glanced at the man waiting in the corner of the room, a sinister presence.

Copeland flicked the end of his cigar into the blue crystal ashtray. "And?"

"Tristan attacked. But the man was trained. As I said, capable. He attacked right back. Broke Tristan's nose. Stabbed him in the leg."

Copeland licked cigar leaf from his teeth with a darting pink tongue. "And?"

"We had to go. Tristan was bleeding. Really bleeding. He'd cut an artery. Fucking blood everywhere. I got him to the car."

Copeland waited.

"He bled out. Died in the back seat. It only took minutes. Tristan is dead."

Another puff of the cigar. "That's unfortunate."

Daniel nodded.

"Who is this lawyer fucking vigilante," said Copeland, trying to keep his voice neutral.

"He said his name was Adam Black."

Another puff. "Where's Tristan?"

"Still in the back seat of my car."

"And where's your car?"

"In my garage."

Copeland drew a heavy sigh. "You're right, Daniel."

"About what?"

"It's a complete fuck-up. What am I to do?"

Daniel said nothing. Copeland regarded him. During the entire exchange, the small secret half smile had never left Daniel's lips. Arrogance? Or perhaps recklessness. This didn't anger Copeland. Quite the opposite. Daniel Pembroke was a psychopath. And extremely dangerous. As such, he was a useful cog in Copeland's organisation. Men like Daniel were a rare breed, and thus a valuable commodity. Copeland needed men like Daniel Pembrose.

"Take care of Tristan," said Copeland.

"Naturally."

Take care. How such little words carried huge implications, thought Copeland. *Take care* meant dismembering, packing, burning, burying – or perhaps sinking. Tristan would either end up in a deep hole in a nameless wood or at the bottom of the sea.

"This Charley Sinclair thing is too exposed. Shut it down. If I recollect, his daughter worked with him during the summer. We therefore have to assume his daughter knows about our... arrangement. Plus this lawyer, Adam Black. Take care of it, Daniel. As I say, shut it down. What do they say in the movies? – no loose ends. Sounds like you might need help." He glanced at the man standing quietly in the corner. "Take Mr Neville. He shows great aptitude in these situations."

"Of course." Daniel's smile drooped. He appeared uncertain. "This morning, when we met the man called Adam Black..."

"Yes?"

"He was... how can I put it... unafraid. Almost as if he enjoyed it. And he was controlled. Sinclair said he was SAS. But he was something else. Something more. His eyes. He had dead eyes."

Copeland gave a cold laugh. "Perhaps you saw something of yourself, Daniel."

Daniel nodded. "I believe I did."

12

The trick is to empty the mind. For that brief period, when you squeeze the trigger, when you stab the blade, and you see the light leaving the enemies eyes, you must learn to feel nothing. No regret, no guilt, no sorrow. And no fear. Effectively gentlemen, you become killing machines. I have a feeling not many of you will have any issues in this regard.

Introductory address given to soldiers of the 22nd Special Air Service Regiment

Black drove straight to his flat after meeting with Charley Sinclair. He lived in a one-bedroomed apartment in a tenement block in the south side of Glasgow. It was small and functional. Black had little need for anything more. He lived a frugal existence. Almost as a penance. Those he loved had died, for which he blamed himself every hour of every day.

He had no television, preferring the radio. He read. He listened to old CDs of music his wife had loved. Beach boys; Simon and Garfunkel; Rolling Stones. He tried not to take too much sugar, drank lots of coffee. Plus, he had a fondness for single malt whisky. In particular, Glenfiddich. Perhaps too much of a fondness. When he got back, it was the first thing he reached for.

He poured a good amount into a glass, and sat on one of two chairs in his living room, facing a bay window. His flat was one up, which meant the view was restricted – the opposite tenement block. Black's mind however was not on the scenery. He sipped the whisky. The taste never diminished. It was early afternoon, the sunshine now gone, hidden behind swollen rain clouds. Suddenly the day was grey, the air heavy.

Black pondered on the events of the morning. Charley Sinclair was in deep shit. He'd mentioned the name Malcolm Copeland. Black had never heard of him. Which didn't surprise – those behind organised crime were usually unknown quantities. Men who coveted their secrecy. Men who could exert power precisely *because* of their secrecy.

Two of Copeland's men had tried to intimidate Sinclair. The front of Black's T-shirt was speckled with Tristan's blood. Too bad. Black wondered if they would return. Possibly. Sinclair was unpredictable. To Copeland, he presented a threat, and as such, was better off dead. The truth was, as soon as Sinclair had agreed to launder money for the mob, he was a dead man. Black had little sympathy. Sinclair was a sleaze and a coward. He had brought this disaster on himself. Black couldn't care less what misfortune befell Charley Sinclair.

Black finished off the glass, reached over, topped up. He settled back, considered.

Sinclair had betrayed his partner, Desmond Gallagher. The logical assumption was that Copeland had orchestrated Gallagher's assassination. Which was a huge play. Gallagher was high profile. Still, it was the obvious move.

As a result of the situation earlier that morning, Black was on the radar. Black sighed, gave a sardonic smile. It was Black's destiny, to find trouble. Perhaps trouble found him. Either way, Black could deal with it. If Copeland came looking, Black wouldn't run. Black took another sip.

If Copeland came looking, Black would come looking right back.

Gallagher's wife, Deborah, had shown him threatening mail from something called the Remus Syndicate. To Black's mind, they were unconnected to Gallagher's murder. Gallagher undoubtedly worked on sensitive cases, stirring reaction from all sorts. The threats were a coincidence. Copeland's involvement was clear and direct. Charley Sinclair told Copeland that Desmond Gallagher knew about the laundering scheme. Copeland had reacted accordingly.

But Black's biggest concern was Deborah. She had asked him – pleaded with him – to find answers. If he told her his suspicions, what then? Nothing good. She would go to the police who, in his opinion, would do little. Malcolm Copeland was undoubtedly connected, to police, politicians, judges. He would have influence with police officers. Organised crime relied on corruption, from top to bottom. Deborah would shout and campaign and create trouble for Malcolm Copeland, who would respond in the only way he knew how. Kill, kill, kill.

Black came to a decision. If he told Deborah, he would be signing her death warrant. Better then to say nothing. Better to forget, and let Desmond Gallagher's death remain a mystery. Not what he would have liked, but then this wasn't his war. Or so he hoped.

He would do nothing for a couple of days, see how it panned out. He would be watchful, and vigilant. If all remained quiet, he would tell Deborah he'd stumbled to a dead end, that she should let it go, let the police handle it. Then, in time, she'd begin to pick up the pieces of her life, and do something Black found impossible.

Move on.

Black nodded to himself. Let sleeping wolves lie, he thought, and eventually the nightmare disappears. Sometimes. But in Black's experience, the nightmare never disappeared.

Better then, to expect the worst. As he had been trained.

Black had preparations to make.

To kill the wolves.

13

Penny Sinclair was twenty-one and a third-year law student at Aberdeen University. Term was ending in a week, then the long summer. She had made a decision. She would stay in Aberdeen. Up until then, during term breaks, she'd stayed some of the time with her dad in Strathaven, some of the time with her mum who lived in Harrogate.

Divorced, her mum and dad hated each other. Penny had given up caring. Though she knew something – she no longer wished to be part of the feud. A pawn in an emotional tug of war. Thus, her decision. She'd rent a flat in Aberdeen with a couple of friends, split the rental three ways. She had a part-time job in a shop. With a student loan it was enough to allow her to survive. Her mum and dad offered to help, but she'd refused. She saw and felt, close up, the shit that divorce could cause. She had a desire to be self-sufficient, relying on no one but herself.

Term was winding down. Exams were over. She was doing an honours course in Oil and Gas Law. Why, she had no real idea, other than a vague notion that because she was in Aberdeen, it might be useful to her some time in the future. But she had no real idea of what she wanted. The law maybe was a road to other things. She was young, with her life before her. Big decisions were for later. Much later.

She had a room in a halls of residence, in the campus of the university. A rather drab building of grey monoblocs, housing a hundred and fifty students. Most had left, back to their homes. The place was eerily quiet. The rooms were silent. The corridors were empty. The end-of-year parties were over. There was little to keep people from leaving. After the angst, the worry, the dread of exams, most wanted to get the hell away.

A week remained until the official end of term. It was Saturday afternoon. Penny worked weekends at a grocery shop a mile from the university. She'd finished the early shift, and was back in her room, lying on her bed, listening to music through headphones. Her friends liked Taylor Swift and Harry Styles. She liked Billy Joel and The Beatles. Her friends scoffed at her "old fashioned" tastes, and called her *eccentric*. Penny scoffed right back, arguing "fashionable" didn't make it good, and *eccentric* was cool. At which they all laughed, including herself.

Her room was small and neat. A desk with a study lamp. A shelf of books. A laptop. On the wall, posters of random things. A bright red pillar box. An enormous daisy. Sunrise on snow-topped mountains. In a corner, a single wardrobe, and next to it, a chest of drawers. A small en suite.

She'd missed a call from her dad that morning. She'd called back, but it had gone straight to voicemail. She hadn't left a message. Her dad had a serious drink problem. Often – always – when he phoned, he was blind drunk. The truth was, it scared her sometimes. He rambled, didn't talk sense. He was bitter. Bitter about his life, about the divorce. She loved him. And she knew he loved her. But she needed distance.

Such thoughts were drifting through her mind, when there was a loud knock on her door. She got up, answered it. Angela Farmer stood in the hallway. Fellow law student, fellow drinking companion, best friend and lover. They had agreed to stay up together. Small, unstoppable. Always cheerful. Her dark hair tied into a fetching topknot. Angela said three words which brought sudden joy to Penny's heart: "Fancy a beer?"

The answer was instant and instinctive.

"Too fucking right."

They made their way to the nearest pub, St Machar's Bar. The beer at the Student Union was cheaper, but St Machar's was special. Close to King's College, it was ancient and intimate. It had an almost witchy feel. Olde worde. Nothing remarkable from the outside. But inside, old stone walls, an ancient hearth carved from hard oak, with a real fire burning bright in the winter, a low ceiling criss-crossed with blackened rafters. On the walls, old photographs of university luminaries. Simple wooden tables and chairs. Nothing pretentious, which was why Penny liked it. It simply existed, unchanging, resolute against the passage of time.

The place was quiet. They got seats by a window. Angela got the drinks. Two bevelled pint tumblers of real ale with a weird Nordic name, impossible to pronounce properly.

She raised her glass. "Here's to fucking *who gives a toss*!"

Penny gave a wry smile. "Fucking who gives a toss?"

Angela grinned. "It was the best I could come up with."

"It's almost poetic."

"I'm a romantic at heart."

"Suits me fine. I'll drink to that."

They clinked glasses, drank. Angela grimaced. "Still tastes like shit."

"Makes sense." Penny pursed her lips. "Having read shit for

the past three years, and listening to shit, a natural progression that we should be tasting it."

"I concur, m'lud," Angela replied in a deep plummy accent, furrowing her eyebrows, assuming a long frown.

Penny copied the expression, pinched her nose, put on a squeaky fluting voice. "Yes, yes, m'lud. I concur too."

"And me, m'lud."

"Me too, m'lud!"

They laughed.

"I mean what the fuck?" said Penny. "I can't imagine us being lawyers. It doesn't compute. All serious and grown up."

"Grown up." Angela nodded like a wise owl.

"I have a theory."

"Which is...?"

"That studying 'The Law...'" Penny uttered "The Law" in a dramatically low voice, "is a slow prelude to death. Like a lingering disease. Like scarlet fever. Or leprosy."

Angela's forehead wrinkled in bemusement. "Leprosy? Interesting analogy. And when does death actually occur, Dr Penny?"

"At the instant a person actually joins a law office. Death, quick and certain. Then years of rigor mortis."

"Bleak outlook," said Angela, "but possibly true."

"I have another theory, which follows on logically from the first."

"Pray tell."

"Think – hidden cameras, a group of lawyers in a room. What have you got?"

"I daren't guess."

"The perfect zombie movie."

Penny raised her glass again. "Here's to death, and then forty years of rigor mortis. And zombies."

"To rigor mortis. And zombies."

Angela took a deep draught, consuming half the contents, then followed with a belch. The bar tender, busy cleaning glasses, glanced up, shook his head, concentrated back on his glasses.

Penny laughed. "Who needs sophistication."

They fell silent. Penny experienced a sudden, inexplicable tinge of melancholy. Perhaps it was the antiquity of the place. Perhaps it was the university term ending. Perhaps it was the missed call from her dad. "He phoned this morning."

"He?"

"Dad."

Angela raised an eyebrow. "Pissed?"

"Probably. Definitely. Obviously. I missed the call. God knows what he wanted. No doubt to impart some rambling nonsensical drunken wisdom no one could ever possibly understand, unless they had a doctorate in inebriation."

"That's quite a sentence. A doctorate in inebriation? Sign me up please."

Penny swallowed some more ale, placed the pint glass down on one of the many cardboard beer mats scattered on the tables.

"He's taken it bad, I think. Who wouldn't? Perhaps, if he stopped drinking and actually spoke to me. You know? Like a father talks to his daughter? His partner's been murdered. His *friend.* Having to run the law firm on his own. And his drinking. His fucking drinking." She took Angela's hand, stroked her skin with the tip of her finger. "I worry about him. Maybe I should do more."

"It's always been a problem, Pen."

"I know. But still..."

"Still... You have a life. He has a life. If you're feeling guilty, then shove it somewhere deep and dark. That's no way to exist. He's your father. Fine. But he's made a choice. And you're you. You're Penny Sinclair, and you've got a life to live. So live it. And right now, we're drinking shitty real ale called some shitty pretentious name in the oldest pub in Aberdeen. What's not to like?"

Penny grinned, drank another mouthful, puckered her lips, made a sour face. "Christ, you're right. It really is shit."

"Of course it is. Otherwise, where's the fun, darling?"

14

Black spent a quiet day on Sunday. He went for a long run, through the streets of Glasgow. Ten miles. The traffic was quiet. He ran at speed. Training in the army, and especially the SAS, had provided a bedrock of fitness, which never really left. He ran every day. Plus press-ups, sit-ups. He went to a cheap, no-frills gym three times a week. He was as fit and strong as a twenty-year-old. His life had been one of relentless physical endurance, ingrained from an early age.

The day was like the one before – dull and overcast. Would they respond? He kept wary, expecting a car to slide up beside him, a window to open. But nothing happened. He got back, showered, fixed some lunch. He sat in his lounge, listened to some music, then went to a local pub, got a whisky, and sat in a corner reading a book. The hours drifted by. Calm before the storm.

Perhaps they wouldn't bother with him. Perhaps they couldn't find him. The name "Adam Black" was not uncommon. Unlikely. Copeland would have resource and money. It was Black's hope that enough damage had been done already, that Copeland would retreat into obscurity, and move on.

~

Monday morning. Black went to work. He rented a somewhat unspectacular office in an area in the south of Glasgow called Shawlands. It was small, comprising a reception room, a toilet, a filing room and an adjacent office where Black worked. It suited him perfectly. He did no advertising. He saw enough clients to pay the bills, and a little extra, which, if he were honest, he was spending too much on single malt whisky.

He employed a secretary, who worked three mornings a week. Karen was brisk and efficient. She organised Black's diary, she typed, answered the phone. A single parent, she needed a flexible and patient boss. He needed someone who could organise. They needed each other. The relationship was perfect.

The morning passed. Karen left at 1pm. She waved him goodbye, through the glass door of his office. He waved back. His diary was free for the rest of the afternoon. Black had a commercial lease to look at. It would take a couple of hours, then he would probably shut shop early. He bought himself a hot pie and a carton of tomato soup. Black had never been fastidious about his diet.

At 2pm two men entered the reception area. One Black recognised immediately. The man called Daniel. He wore an elegant pale blue cotton suit, a white shirt, open at the collar. He could have been dressed for a summer stroll. The other, Black did not know. Tall, possibly six four. A clear two inches taller than Black. Balding, tanned, his face all lines and hard ridges. Thick neck, strong shoulders. Sombre in a dark pinstripe suit, dark tie. Casual violence emanated from both men. Black had confronted such men many times before, and recognised them for what they were. Killers. Pure and simple.

Black saw them through his glass door. They saw him. Daniel raised his hand in an airy gesture of greeting. They politely knocked, and entered the room. Black was sitting behind his desk.

They stood before him. Daniel still maintained his little half smile, as if he found the situation mildly amusing.

"I hadn't realised you gentlemen had an appointment," said Black.

"Excuse us, Mr Black. We hoped you wouldn't mind. Given the nature of our business."

"It's a little awkward. I'm a busy man. Why don't you telephone my secretary tomorrow morning, and we'll schedule you in for later in the week."

"That would be inconvenient," replied Daniel, his voice soft, reasonable. "Now would seem an excellent opportunity to continue our discussion."

Black essayed an easy smile. "Remind me – what discussion was this?"

"Don't you recall? The one commenced on Saturday morning. And the one I hope to conclude this afternoon."

"I understand completely. Aren't you going to introduce me?"

Daniel nodded. "Of course. How remiss. My full name's Daniel Pembrose. My colleague here is Mr Neville. To be honest, I don't know his first name. Isn't that bizarre? He likes to keep things on a strictly formal basis. Also, as you may have noticed, he's not a man who enjoys conversation."

"Not everyone's a chatterbox."

"Indeed not. You and Mr Neville have things in common. He served in the armed forces. With the Royal Marines, to be precise. After that, a few years with the French Foreign Legion. He is a most... how can I say... capable man. Tristan would have enjoyed being here, to rekindle the relationship. Sadly he is unable to attend."

"Sorry to hear that," said Black. "Hope it's not serious."

"Terminal. You had the misfortunate to kill him."

"Sad news. Please pass on my condolences. He was a charming man, from beginning to end."

"Charm was not his foremost quality, though he had many others. But we're not here to discuss him. My employer has asked us to tie up loose ends. His words, I might add."

"Loose ends? That's a rather hackneyed expression. You should tell your boss to read more. How many ends do you intend to tie, I wonder."

The serene smile never left Daniel's lips. Black wondered if he had ever encountered a more sinister presence.

"I'm glad you asked, because it's important you understand what your actions have caused. Your 'client', Charley Sinclair, is dead. He took his own life last night. With a little assistance from us. We... how can I put it... sent him on his way. He's hanging from the bannisters in his stairs. A sorry situation."

"Tragic."

"You'll know he has a daughter?"

Black said nothing.

"I'll take that as a yes. That *hackneyed expression* you mentioned, includes her, I'm afraid. She's another loose end. Tonight, two of my friends will be paying her a visit, in Aberdeen. See the damage you've caused, Mr Black. May I call you Adam?"

"Mr Black's fine. You like the sound of your own voice, Daniel. But it grates a little after a while. You said you had business to conclude. I'm getting a tad bored. And I think Frankenstein's monster beside you feels the same way. He's beginning to drool. Why don't we move on, and finish our business. It would be nice to see this to its proper conclusion."

The edges of Daniel's mouth curled downward, crescent-shaped. "I'm enjoying the moment, Mr Black," he said quietly. "But you're right. Tick tock. Time to die."

He showed his sad twisted little smile, turned his head a fraction towards the man called Mr Neville, from which he seemed to derive precise information. Neville unbuttoned the front of his jacket, pulled out a pistol – specifically a Beretta.

"Bon voyage," said Daniel.

"Au revoir sounds more romantic," responded Black. A sudden deafening blast. Neville lurched back, shrieking. His right leg was gone, just below the hip. Blown off. In its place, a straggle of veins, blood and torn cloth. Black had given him the full payload of a sawn-down shotgun, fastened to the underside of his desk.

Daniel took a step back, hand reaching under his jacket. Black didn't hesitate. He rolled across the desk, papers scattering. He leapt onto Daniel. They tumbled to the floor. Daniel got to his feet, a semi-automatic in his right hand. Black rose, slapped it to one side, skewing his aim. A sound like a firecracker, as it punched a bullet into the wall.

Black seized Daniel's wrist. Another shot, as a bullet punctured a filing cabinet. Daniel hacked at Black's neck with his free hand. Black raised his shoulder, absorbing the blow. Black brought his head down, butting Daniel's nose and upper jaw. Daniel staggered, disoriented, the pistol slipping from his fingers. Black swung a punch. Daniel, expertly, caught Black's arm, attempted a lock, the aim to snap the ulna. Black anticipated, relaxed his arm, brought his weight round, twisted free, kicking Daniel's knee.

Daniel grunted in pain, but reacted instantly, driving a fist into Black's face. It was like being hit with a sledgehammer. Black reeled. Daniel stooped for the pistol. Black stepped forward, kicked it away. Daniel lunged, rugby tackled Black. They fell to the ground. Daniel tried to get on top. Black relaxed, augmented the momentum, got on top of Daniel, punched him on the larynx. Daniel spluttered, choking, tried to struggle free.

Black manoeuvred, pinning Daniel's arms down with his knees, caught his neck in the crook of his arm, squeezed. Daniel's movements lessened, became still. Black stood, light-headed, breathing deeply. Daniel was unconscious, but not dead. Black retrieved the pistol.

During the commotion, Daniel's colleague – Mr Neville – had dragged himself to the office door, blood trailing behind him like slime from a snail. His effort had been in vain. He lay unmoving, pale and dead, life drained onto Black's carpet.

Black went to the smashed filing cabinet, opened a bottom drawer, pulled out a bottle of Glenfiddich, drank straight from the bottle.

Tough day at the office.

And it wasn't over.

15

Jason Drummond, forty-five, was head of security for Rosewood Hospital. Plus a lot more. He'd enlisted with the armed services at sixteen, joining the Royal Marine Commandos. Was selected for the Special Boat Service. Made his way up the ranks, to Major, at the age of thirty-three. During the journey he got his black belt in judo, and became a Brigade boxing champion, middleweight.

At thirty-four, he was dishonourably discharged. An altercation with a civilian in a pub in Plymouth. He broke the man's jaw. The problem was, he didn't stop, and broke both his arms and punctured a lung. When Drummond started a job, he liked to finish it. The episode was hushed up. But Drummond was given the boot.

He used his talents and got a job working for a private security firm in Qatar, then Iraq, then various locations in Africa. His job description – Security Consultant. The reality – mercenary. He killed without compunction, which made him useful. Certain organisations found such a trait a worthwhile investment.

Including the Rosewood Hospital. Or more particularly, the Remus Syndicate.

Drummond was in his office, pondering his past, and how he'd arrived at his present situation. He was quietly pleased with himself. He'd started with nothing. Now he had over two million in cash in a safety deposit box. And the way it was going, his pot would increase at an almost geometric rate. He got a five per cent cut in the profits. Which meant, for every live body brought safely, he collected a small fortune.

His office was in a separate annex in the hospital grounds, a mile from the main hospital building, a place strictly out of bounds save for those in the inner sanctum. A two-level building, nondescript, shrouded by heavy trees and high bushes. Invisible to the casual observer. His office was on the first floor. Beneath, the operating rooms.

The room was functional. A clock on the wall, a calendar, a desk, a laptop, a telephone, and little else. Drummond disliked clutter. The phone was for internal calls only. If he required to make a call to the outside, he was careful to use a burner.

Which was what he used now, to speak to his Turkish contact. The man called Bustan. He connected a simple voice modulating device, made the call.

As ever, Bustan answered immediately. It was in his interests to be readily accessible.

"We still on target for Tuesday?"

Bustan's rumbling voice answered. "Of course. It's been set up. As you wanted. Three kids. No adults."

"Make it four," said Drummond.

"Four kids?"

"What the fuck do you think I mean? Fucking peanuts?"

"This is short notice. Do you know how complicated it is to set this up?"

"And this is my problem? You like the money, so fucking earn it. Am I clear?"

A silence followed. He fancied he could hear the gears in Bustan's mind click and whirr, digesting the new parameters, calculating the profits. The hospital only paid for the merchandise delivered. The extra children would part way compensate for the loss of the adults. Which meant more pound sterling – both for Bustan and himself.

Bustan, the consummate merchant, answered in the positive, as Drummond knew he would.

"Of course. Of course. Four kids. Not easy, but possible. Yes. Very possible."

"Good. Get it done."

Drummond hung up, destroyed the phone. An extra child. A simple phone call, and he'd made a sizeable increase in his pay packet.

Drummond sat back.

If he could organise a hundred kids, he would do it. The way he saw it, the Remus Syndicate – with his assistance – was simply following a basic rule of economics. Supply and demand.

The demand, which never stopped, was for something most precious.

And the Syndicate were perfectly placed to supply it. And the commodity was such, they could name their price.

Which they did.

16

We do not condone the use of torture.
Official statement by The British Army

We never torture prisoners to get information.
We merely ask them in a forthright manner.
Unofficial statement by Staff Sergeant
to new recruits of the 22nd Special Air
Service Regiment

Black had locked the door of his office, plus the main door at the front of the building. He was on the first floor of a two-storey block. The unit below him was a vacant beauty salon, with its own entrance. The other entrance at street level was exclusive to Black, opening to a rather austere hall, a set of stairs, going directly up to Black's office. There was also a back door, again for his exclusive use, leading out to a secluded and single private parking bay, where Black kept his car.

At that moment, privacy was a top concern.

Before him, sitting on a chair meant for clients, was the man called Daniel Pembroke. Black had prepared for such an eventuality. He had removed Daniel's jacket and strapped his wrists to the armrests of the chair with heavy-duty industrial sealing tape. Also, his calves and ankles to the front wooden legs.

On his desk, plugged to a socket by a four-foot cable, was a handheld heat gun, designed to strip paint, the end of which glowed orange red.

Black's time was limited. He got a kettle of cold water, splashed it on Daniel's face, slapped him on the cheeks. Daniel stirred, grunted. His eyes opened, blinked, rolled in his head, as he tried to adjust to his situation. His first reaction was to jostle his arms free. He desisted, realising he was bound in, any effort to escape futile.

Once he had come to terms with his predicament, the serene half-smile returned. Black was mildly impressed by his composure.

"I hope you're comfortable," said Black.

"I'd be more comfortable if you unstrapped me from this chair."

"Maybe later. We have things to discuss."

"What will you do with me?"

"That depends entirely on you. You are – how can I say – master of your own destiny."

"You have a way with words, Mr Black."

"Thank you. You're very kind. However, we must press on."

Black pulled the curtains of the single window. He switched on a portable CD player he had placed on the floor. Rolling Stones greatest hits. His wife's favourite. He pulled up a chair, and sat opposite Daniel.

"This is cosy." Daniel swivelled his head round, to the office door. Black hadn't bothered moving Neville's body. He lay in a pond of blood, face pale and stricken.

"Mr Neville lost his footing," said Black.

Daniel shrugged. "Careless."

Black continued, "You work for Malcolm Copeland. I'd like to pay him a visit. Where would I find him?"

Daniel took a deep breath, regarded Black with eyes like flint. "Mr Copeland covets his privacy. He is almost obsessive about it."

"Of course he is. And who can blame him? Nevertheless, please answer the question."

Daniel sighed, said nothing.

Black nodded. "Looks like a little persuasion is required."

"Persuasion?" Daniel glanced at the heat gun. "You intend to burn me with that thing?"

"Not quite." Black got up, opened a drawer in his desk, took out a pair of handheld metal shears. He returned to his chair.

"More like cauterise. Don't want you bleeding all over the carpet, like your friend, Mr Neville. There's enough mess already. I believe you're left-handed. Yes?"

Daniel didn't respond. His face was tight and pale. His smile had gone. His hand was clenched into a fist. Black was undeterred. He manoeuvred the blades between the fingers, so they rested round the index finger, next to the knuckle joint. He reached over, got the heat gun, held it poised.

"I'll ask again. Where will I find Malcolm Copeland?"

Daniel cocked his head, as if trying to fathom whether Black was serious. "You're deluded. His house is a fortress. He has bodyguards. You're one man. Don't you understand who you're dealing with?"

"Wrong answer."

Black squeezed the handle of the shears. The blades, designed to cut sheet metal, snipped smoothly through flesh, blood, bone, all to the sound of "Jumpin' Jack Flash". Daniel released a short sharp burst of pain. Black pressed the red-hot nozzle of the heat gun against the open wound. Skin sizzled. Daniel gave a low moan.

"Oops," said Black. "I think that was your trigger finger. Not to worry. Plenty more. Now, Daniel, be a sport and answer the question."

Daniel took several short breaths. Eventually he spoke. "He'll kill me."

Black shook his head. "That's theoretical. This is real. This is happening. Let's go for pinkie."

Black adjusted the shears, repeated the process, amputating, cauterising. Daniel moaned. Two of his fingers lay on the floor.

"Three's the charm. Let's try the thumb. What's it to be?"

Daniel licked his lips. His skin shone with sweat. He swallowed, found his voice. "Malcolm Copeland is a dangerous man. You have no conception of what he is capable of."

"Wrong again. Don't think you're getting the hang of this, old sport."

A third cut, the air smelling of singed flesh.

Black sat back. The man before him was not the same man who had entered his office an hour earlier. The sanguine smile had gone. His face was bereft of colour. His hair clung to his scalp. His body seemed to have shrunk inside his suit. He sat, hunched, head bowed, saliva trailing from the side of his mouth.

"You've lost three fingers," said Black. "For what? An address. I wonder if Malcolm Copeland would do the same for you."

Daniel stirred, looked up. He stared at Black. His eyes shone, with fear and pain. Black knew what he was thinking – what's next?

Black continued, spoke in an almost breezy voice. "I don't think the finger *thing* is working. You've heard of gelding?"

The muscles worked on either side of Daniel's jaw. *He's picturing a scene*, thought Black. *And he's not liking it.*

"Of course you have. They geld horses. Otherwise known as castration. You've heard of castration, surely."

Daniel's eyes remained fixed on Black, his skin stretched tight over his cheekbones.

Black sighed. "Such a shame to ruin a good pair of trousers." He crouched over, started to cut the cloth, from the waist down.

"Enough," whispered Daniel.

Black continued cutting, creating a clean tear down the crotch area. He pulled the cloth to one side, exposing dark blue underwear. Gently, he started to snip away the material.

Daniel took another wheezy breath, and spoke. "He lives two miles outside a town called Biggar. In a fucking mansion, called Millard House. Take the sign for Blackwater Reservoir. You'll find it easy enough. You can't fucking miss it." He licked the edges of his mouth with the tip of his tongue. "I sincerely hope you die in the process, Black."

Black sat back. "See how easy that was? You could have saved three fingers. But I guess a man's dick is more important. Shame you're left-handed. You'll have to practise with your right. And is he there now?"

"That's his main home. He's staying there until this whole fucking thing goes away."

Black gave a thin-lipped smile. "Goes away. I like that expression. It covers a wide range. Including the murder of me, Charley Sinclair, and Sinclair's daughter."

Daniel said nothing, sullen and scared.

"And Desmond Gallagher. Did you kill him? Or did Copeland order someone else to do it."

Daniel swallowed, licked his lips as he formulated his response. "It wasn't me. Copeland is a secretive man. I don't know anything about that."

Black believed him. Daniel was broken, and talking freely.

"Charley's daughter," said Black. "Penny? What were your plans for her?"

"Two-man team. We know where she lives."

"And?"

Daniel spoke, his voice low, almost a murmur. "She has a room at the halls of residence. They would take her somewhere remote, kill her, and bury her deep. She'd never be found. Or maybe just kill her on the spot. Who knows."

"I understand," said Black. "Tying up loose ends. Makes sense. Which halls?"

"What are you – her knight in shining armour? Excuse me while I puke. You and I are not much different. You really think you can save her, Black?"

"What I think is irrelevant to you. Which halls?"

"Fyfe Halls. Room 125."

"Thank you. That wasn't so difficult."

Black stood.

"What now?" Daniel said. "You going to kill me? I gave you what you wanted."

"You did. For which I'm grateful."

Daniel blinked. Sweat dribbled down his face. "You'll let me go?"

Black gave a wintry grin. "In a manner of speaking. I assume you were to contact Copeland after you'd completed business here."

"That would be the normal course of events."

"Excellent."

Black reached over, searched Daniel, found his mobile phone in his inside jacket pocket.

"What do you intend to do?"

"I would like your assistance. You're going to tell your boss that you've killed me. Easy, yes? What's the password? If you wouldn't mind."

Daniel gave him a set of numbers. Black tapped the screen, found Contacts.

"MC?"

Daniel nodded.

"Thank you."

Black tapped the screen again. A voice answered, immediately.

The voice, so Black assumed, of Malcolm Copeland.

17

Dr Michael Stapleton's office was large and bright, and comprised a section of the top floor. An entire wall was glass, and the view beyond, a landscape of woodland and lush fields, and in the far distance, the flat grey surface of the sea. On the opposite wall, a six feet by six feet painting – an abstract swirl of bright intense colour. *Whirlwind.* An original piece. On another wall, glass units containing cups and trophies, gleaming in the sunshine. Stapleton had been a rugby player in his youth, had won two caps for Scotland while at Edinburgh University studying for his medical degree. Also, dotted on the walls like pimples on a pale skin, certificates and awards.

Stapleton was an achiever. Regarded as one of the top surgeons in the country, and he had about every qualification to prove it. He was rich, and he liked being rich. He liked to spend. He liked to acquire *things.* Cars, paintings, jewellery, objets d'art. He had several properties around the world. His latest, a villa in Tenerife. He was single and had no interest in sex. With either women or men. Buying a French sculpture, or a piece of Italian furniture gave him an orgasm. He lacked empathy, and he knew it. Which, to his mind, was an essential quality in a surgeon – and a prerequisite for the darker path he travelled.

The office was split into two sections. At one end, a large desk cleverly constructed of wood, metal and glass. There were no paper files. Everything was committed to software. On the desktop, two delicate horse sculptures, crafted from a wire armature, followed by numerous applications of resin clay, varnished with soft black acrylic paint. Stapleton paid £5,000 for each one, on a whim. Also, a bronze art deco sculpture of a prowling jaguar, rough-hewn, commissioned by Stapleton at a cost of £3,000. Other items were placed at specific points. Altogether, Stapleton had over £20,000 worth of desktop ornaments.

At the other side of the room, an expansive couch of Italian cream leather, with three contrasting black leather chairs, an ivory-framed coffee table, and on an antique side cabinet, a complicated looking coffee machine. In a corner, a drinks cabinet of heavy dark wood. On the far wall, a large screen.

Stapleton fixed himself a vodka and fresh orange, sat on the couch facing the screen. He tapped a button on a remote control on the armrest. The screen flickered. Suddenly, a face materialised. A Chinese man. Round fleshy face, softly waving black hair, limpid blue eyes. His name was Xing Chen. Known as the "The Broker". The link between Stapleton and massive wealth. As such, a man to keep happy.

Chen spoke, dispensing with pleasantries. His voice was tinny, and harsh. His English was perfect.

"We can't have a repeat performance, Michael. If it happens again, we lose face. Our reputation suffers. You understand this?"

"Of course. But your clients have to appreciate, to an extent, this is a lottery. We work with what we are given. There is no way we could have predicted the parents both had cancer."

Chen's face remained impassive. To read the man was like trying to read a piece of wood. Stapleton had given up long ago.

"This is not my problem," Chen said. "That's your end. Deadlines are strict in this game. And the merchandise has to be quality. The process is, how you would say… time sensitive. Yes? If you can't deliver, then the consequences are exact. We look elsewhere."

"We've got it sorted," replied Stapleton, his voice like silk. "Tell your clients there will be no more delays. The last situation was… unfortunate, and unforeseen. But will not be repeated."

Chen gave the slightest nod. "This is reassuring. I will convey your words. Is there anything else you need to tell me?"

Stapleton raised an eyebrow. "Sorry?"

"There's no danger of Remus being compromised?"

"The problem's gone away. As you know, Desmond Gallagher is dead."

"He has records. Files. Now with the police, I imagine."

"He has nothing. They have nothing, I promise. His case was built on supposition and rumour. His death was… timely. He's gone. The problem's gone with him."

"Gallagher is dead. But that doesn't mean the problem's gone away. You're making an assumption. I can't afford assumptions. Neither can you. In China, we deal with things in a certain way. Call it *absolutism*, if you want."

Stapleton frowned. "Absolutism?"

"Gallagher worked in a law firm. He had colleagues. He had a family. Absolutism, Michael. Burn everything he touched. No traces. Burn everything to the ground. Scorched earth, yes?"

Chen's expression remained inscrutable. His image vanished. The screen went black. The meeting was over.

Stapleton sipped his drink, pondered.

He couldn't blame Chen for feeling anxious. Things had been difficult lately. Desmond Gallagher's relentless pursuit into the activities of the hospital had been uncomfortable for them. But Gallagher was dead. The subsequent issue was the corrupted merchandise, which had cost them a vast amount of money. That, Stapleton resolved, would never happen again. But the whole thing put together didn't look good.

Lose face. Chen's words. Stapleton couldn't allow that to happen.

Absolutism. Chen had a point. Wise, even. No traces.

He finished his drink, got his mobile, tapped the screen, and spoke to the man who was adept at such things.

Jason Drummond, his head of security, answered immediately. "Yes?"

"Our Chinese broker is nervous. About the Desmond Gallagher affair. What do you know about absolutism?"

A silence, then Drummond responded, "Everything."

18

Malcolm Copeland, as a matter of habit, always had three men stationed in and around his country mansion. Since the debacle with Charley Sinclair, and the death of Tristan, he felt it wise to escalate his security. Perhaps a sixth sense, honed over many years of gangland experience. An instinct that trouble was looming.

Also, Copeland was a man who did his homework. Adam Black. More than a mere lawyer. Had to be, to deal with Tristan with such apparent ease. One thing Copeland had learned in his trade of extortion, blackmail and murder – never, ever underestimate the enemy.

He asked discreet questions. He had friends in the police force. Friends who would do anything for a thick envelope of cash. Also, Copeland checked the internet. The man called Adam Black was more than a lawyer. Much more. Ex-SAS, counterterrorism, battle hardened. Achieving a modicum of fame for rescuing the prime minister's daughter some years back. In essence, a real fucking handful.

Copeland didn't like such men interfering in his life. Daniel said he would handle the matter. Take care of Black. Daniel was reliable, and talented. He killed with clinical efficiency, and enjoyed doing it. But Copeland couldn't take any chances. Doubts fluttered in his mind.

Adam Black. A real fucking handful. Copeland thought it wise to double the manpower. Six men. Three men in the gardens, three inside. Capable and experienced.

Copeland was in the sub level of his house. The foundations hollowed out, and converted into a heated swimming pool, jacuzzi, sauna and showers. A half-million-pound refit. He didn't swim. His daughters, ten and twelve, were splashing about in the pool with two other kids. Invited for a stay over. His wife, Candice, was lying stretched on a padded recliner at the pool side, glass of crisp cold Chablis beside her. Lean and tanned. She used her treadmill every day.

Copeland fucked her once a week, which was about the extent of his exercise, and even then, the activity was short. But she liked his money, and she had her kids, so she would never complain. Occasionally, Copeland dabbled with prostitutes. He liked them young. Really young. And he liked it rough. A few times, in his youth, he'd gone too far, but who cared about dead whores.

He was sitting in the jacuzzi, legs floating in a bed of warm bubbles. At his elbow, a glass of Glenmorangie. His doctors told him to stay away from the stuff. His attitude was fuck the doctors. There was a pill for everything. Beside the glass, his mobile phone. He was waiting for the message. The text to say – *loose end removed.* But the phone stayed silent.

He got up, his belly huge and glistening fish-white. He finished the whisky, scooped up his mobile, padded along the pool side. He smiled at the kids. He stopped at his wife. "You want a top-up?"

"I'm fine."

He made his way out of the pool area, dressed in pink and

yellow swimming trunks, fat quivering jelly-like with every step. He got a towel, wrapped it round his shoulders, made his way up wide carpeted stairs, emerged into a long hallway, walls gleaming with vintage oak panelling. He opened a door, entered his study, his wet feet creating footprints on the carpet. He sat by his desk, tossed the mobile on the mahogany surface.

He took deep breaths, each inhalation tinged with the slightest wheeze. The walk up the stairs had caused his heart to hammer. Perhaps he should install a lift. He stared at the phone, willing it to vibrate into life.

He was uneasy. He didn't like this feeling. With his money and influence, he should be insulated from any form of jeopardy.

Adam Black. The man was a concern. The whole thing was a fuck-up. The rules were simple in this game. Charley Sinclair had become a liability. Copeland had to assume he'd mouthed off, to Black, and his daughter, Penny Sinclair. Copeland knew she was a law student, had worked with her father sometimes for summer pocket money. Charley Sinclair may have confided in her, warned her.

When you entered Copeland's world, there were consequences. His rules weren't so different from the rules of ancient warfare. Destroy the enemy, and everything about the enemy. Killing the source wasn't enough. The tentacles had to be dismembered and crushed. To avoid reprisals. A son or daughter harbouring a grudge, and looking for payback years down the line.

The daughter would be gone this evening. Adam Black, however. Daniel was to text, as soon as it was done. So far, silence. Copeland didn't like silence. He picked up the phone, pressed the keypad, speed-dialled Daniel's number. Straight to voice message. Copeland hung up.

Adam Black. Ex-special services. A killer.

Fuck it. Black was no different from any number of hard nuts who'd had the misfortune to cross Copeland. And Copeland's answer had always been swift and devastating,

And yet...

Adam Black.

Copeland had an instinct for things.

Perhaps Black was different.

Perhaps Black had his own game. And his own set of rules.

Then his phone buzzed. He picked up.

It was Daniel.

19

Black had the phone on loudspeaker, placed it close to Daniel's mouth. He gestured to Daniel to speak. He held the Beretta in his other hand, the barrel pressed against the side of Daniel's head.

Malcolm Copeland spoke. "Daniel?"

"It's done," said Daniel, voice leaden. "Black is dead."

Silence.

"Sure he is. Is he there? With a gun at your head? Put him on."

Daniel looked at Black, waiting for instruction. Black shrugged. It had been a long shot, but worth the try.

"It's good to talk," he said. "And to answer your question, yes, I have a gun at Daniel's head. The other man you sent to kill me, Mr Neville, is now ex Mr Neville, who at this very moment is making a dreadful mess of my carpet."

Copeland responded with a harsh metallic chuckle. "Send me the bill. It hardly matters. Nothing changes."

"Not from my perspective. Daniel has been most talkative. He likes a good conversation. How about this. I'll make a proposition. I'll allow Daniel to walk out of my office, in relatively one piece. You cancel your Aberdeen excursion."

Another pause, then, "Daniel should really learn to be more discreet. As I said, Mr Black, nothing changes. The Aberdeen excursion is bought and paid for. There's a young lady there we're meeting. And of course, we're keen to see you again. To complete our business with you."

"Good. I'm glad we got that out the way." Black turned, shot Daniel in the head, all to the sound of Mick Jagger belting out "Sympathy for the Devil". Daniel and the chair toppled over in a sudden bright geyser of blood.

Black continued, "Daniel will be much more discreet in future, now that his brains complement my office décor. I don't care about the girl. You go ahead and do what you have to do. But here's the situation. You sent two men to kill me. Now they're both dead. Guess what? I enjoyed it. You might think I'm at a disadvantage, because I've stumbled into your world, where bad men do bad things. A world you might think I cannot possibly understand. You are so wrong. You've entered my world. Where you confront a new nightmare. Me. Where I don't stop. Where you keep looking over your shoulder, day and night. Until the day comes when I rip your fucking heart out."

Black hung up.

He had work to do, and a journey to make.

The line went dead. Copeland stared into space. Daniel had just been shot. Black had performed the act, casually, without compunction. If a man can do that, he thought, then he was capable of anything. Black had issued a threat. Copeland wasn't used to being threatened. Fear and intimidation was his game, one he had excelled at, and from which he had earned significant wealth. Suddenly, he had a flavour of the other side. The victim's side.

A feeling fluttered in his stomach. One he rarely experienced. Dread.

Black had made his intentions clear. Fair enough. If the bastard wanted a war, then he'd get one. Doubt whispered in his mind. Perhaps six men weren't enough.

Perhaps a thousand men weren't enough, for someone like Adam Black.

20

Penny Sinclair tried to phone her father, but got straight to voicemail. Despite Angela's lecture, she *did* feel guilty. His drinking was bad, always had been, but lately it was shit bad. He hinted of problems, of issues, but when she pushed, he clammed up, tight as a drum, and drank more. And now, with his partner murdered, the whole episode splashed across every front page, she couldn't begin to fathom the pressure he was under.

But he was an alcoholic. Perhaps worse – he was an alcoholic in denial. It wouldn't matter what she said or did. Her father found consolation from only one source – a gin bottle. Or indeed any bottle. This thought eased Penny's conscience, but not by much.

It was mid-afternoon, and the shop was quiet. Her shift finished at six. There were only two of them working. Herself and an older woman, who took breaks every hour to have a sly puff in the backyard beside the rubbish bins. Penny didn't mind. She found the work almost therapeutic after the slog of law exams.

She worked the till, inventoried the stock, cleaned the

fridges, scoured the ovens. The place was a general grocery shop, selling over-the-counter hot and cold food, pastries, tea, coffee. Penny would work here during the summer, earning enough to pay rent and electric and food. Plus a little more for beer money.

The evening was planned. Back to halls of residence when her shift finished. Shower, change, get ready. Angela would come round for eight. They might open some chilled white wine. Talk. Then the pub, to meet more friends for nine. The university pubs would be quiet, term all but finished. They would venture into the town centre. Maybe a pub crawl. Maybe a club. Angela would stay the night. Penny was looking forward to it.

She finished work. Another girl came in to replace her. She meandered back, a distance of just over a mile, still in her work uniform. It was early evening, and warm. The university buildings looked solemn and sad in the long shadows. Gone, the bustle and energy of young people, cutting about like a million fish in a shifting current. The place seemed hollow and empty, the air tinged with melancholy.

She tried her father again. Straight to voice message. She almost phoned her mother. She spoke to her once a week. The conversations were usually one-sided – her mother did the talking, Penny did the listening. Her mother had found a new partner, a new life. Everything was wonderful and happy. Penny had been demoted to a peripheral. Up until then, she'd flitted between her parents during holidays. The divorce had been tangled and bitter. She was fed up with both of them. She had her own life to live.

But it didn't stop her from worrying. For her father.

Something was wrong. He drank like a man who wanted to die. He spoke like a man who was scared.

She got back to the halls. The building was almost empty. She too would be moving out in a couple of days, to a new flat. Her room was on the top floor. There was no lift. The stairs were wide, the steps grey concrete, the walls white peeling plaster. She got to her corridor. Long and drab, the walls the same white plaster, doors on either side, running the entire length. Fifty rooms, twenty-five on each side. Illuminated by harsh strip lights. She got to her room. Number 125.

She rummaged for her key, unlocked the door, entered. She tossed her holdall on the bed, went to the small en suite, switched the shower on. She tried her father again. Answer machine. *Fuck it*, she thought. He was doubtless on a bender. She tossed her phone on the bed beside her holdall, started to strip, wondering what she should wear, her mind on the night ahead.

21

Black was prepared. He wrapped the man called Mr Neville – complete with detached leg – in a large blanket. He carried him out and downstairs to the back courtyard, to his car. The going was slow, and awkward. The dead were always heavy. He popped open the boot, dropped him in. There was a chance someone might have seen, but the chance was slim. The courtyard was secluded, and private.

Black had to move quickly. He bounded back up the stairs, back into his office. He cut away the tape holding Daniel to the chair. He rolled to the floor, his small secret smile now permanently fixed. Black searched his pockets, found a wallet with two hundred pounds, and a collection of credit cards. He kept the money. Cash was of little consequence to the departed.

Black then repeated the process, wrapping the body in a blanket, taking it downstairs, placing him in the boot with his dead friend. He went back upstairs, changed into a fresh shirt and pair of jeans. The carpet he would clean later. He'd brought a sports bag, in which he placed the pistols, plus the shotgun he'd used to blow off Mr Neville's right leg. Black locked the main front door of his office. Karen wasn't due in the next day.

Enough scope, he hoped, to return and clean up. If his luck held out, of course, and the ability to return was an option.

It was 3pm. It would take two and a half hours to get to Aberdeen. He'd hit rush hour, so it could take longer. He had no choice. If he called the police, and tried to explain assassins were set to kill a law student at the university, they'd think he was mad. A prank call. In the unlikely event they did react, it would be hours before they roused themselves to do anything. Her killers would merely lay low, and wait for their chance. He got in his car, placed the sports bag on the passenger seat, drove out of Glasgow, heading north, with two dead men in his boot. He would dispose of them later.

He drove, careful to keep well within the speed limits. The road to Aberdeen was cursed with average-speed cameras. He was going blind, with no real plan formulated. He had an address. Get there. Then work it out. If he were too late, and the girl was gone, then... He refused to speculate.

Daniel, in his last moments, had described him, somewhat sarcastically, as a knight in shining armour. His armour consisted of two Berettas he had taken from the dead men in his boot. He was no knight. He was a killer. Trained to end life. With his hands, with knives, with guns. With anything.

A knight in shining armour? The opposite, thought Black ruefully. A machine, efficient at killing. Something he had a special talent for.

Something he enjoyed.

22

7.30pm. A knock at the door. Penny Sinclair was lying on her bed, listening to some old Fleetwood Mac through headphones, reading a John Grisham novel. She heard the knock, despite the music. Angela was early, a rare occurrence. Being punctual would have been a minor miracle, but a half-hour early? Penny was impressed. Angela was keen for a solid drinking session. Fair enough.

Penny removed her headphones, got up. She hadn't yet changed, and was wearing a fluffy white dressing gown. Another knock, louder. "Okay, okay."

She opened the door. Two men stood before her. Dark suits, dark ties. She gasped, stepped back.

"Penny Sinclair?" said one. He was tall, hair cropped into a boyish crew cut, flat hard features. The other was smaller, but broad and square. They were out of place, in this building, in the grounds of the university. They belonged in another world, dominated by violence and terror.

Her mouth was dry. She nodded.

"Perfect," said the man. She could smell cologne. He unbuttoned his jacket. Strapped to his side, a holster, and in it, a gun. He pulled it out. She tried to speak, but was unable to articulate.

The smaller man stepped back. The other raised his arm, pointed. A sound, like a sharp cough. Once, twice. Suddenly, her chest felt constricted. Her insides imploded, squeezing her lungs, compressing her heart.

She staggered back. She felt herself falling. The world rose up. The room whirled. There was no pain. Her breath was caught. She saw things with sudden bright clarity. The two men entered her room, stood gazing down at her. She saw them turn, saw the shock on their faces.

Another had entered the room.

Black got to the university, parked the car close to its centre. He had no idea of the location of Penny's building. The place was quiet. Term had finished, he assumed. A wisp of dread fluttered in his stomach. The traffic had been slow when he'd reached Aberdeen, reduced to a frustrating crawl. He spotted a couple of young men, sports bags strapped over their shoulder. Looked like they were heading to the gym. He asked for directions. *Sure.* They pointed to a large building of blond sandstone and high arched stained-glass windows, peaked dark slate roof. *Other side of the chapel. Past the green.*

Black thanked them, jogged along a grey flagstoned walkway which snaked round the chapel building. Beyond, an area of grass, neatly mown, dotted with brightly coloured wooden benches. In its centre, a three-level fountain, water falling like a soft murmur. Black saw the halls – a rather drab featureless flat-roofed building of grey mono blocks and rows and columns of small square windows, reminiscent of something straight from Communist Russia.

He ran across the lawn, past the fountain, reached the entrance. There was no communal lock. People could enter and exit as they wished. He knew her number. On a wall, a fire safety plan. She was on the third level. He raced up the stairs, opened a swing glass fire door. He entered a corridor, doors on either side. There! Two men, standing briefly in the hall, then entering a room. Instinct cut in. These men were wrong.

He pulled out the Beretta from his jacket pocket sprinted a distance of thirty feet, got to the room. The two men, their backs to him, stood looking down at a figure, stricken, lying on the floor. They spun round. One held a pistol – a Glock 46. He aimed it at Black. Too late. Black crouched, fired, all in one fluid movement, exactly as he'd been trained. The man's throat seemed to expand in a sparkle of bright blood. The other tried to draw his pistol. Another shot, the noise booming in the close confines. The man took it in the chest. He staggered back. Black fired a third time. The man's head snapped back, brains spattered on the back wall like flicks of wet paint.

Black strode forward, knelt to the girl on the floor. The front of her dressing gown was saturated. She tried to speak.

"No," said Black softly. "There's no need." He cradled her head on his lap. She opened her mouth, coughed up a volume of blood. Black held her. She gave one last gasping breath, a small desperate shudder, and Penny Sinclair died in Black's arms.

23

Black left Penny where she lay. There was nothing further to be done. He closed the door gently behind him. The corridor was quiet and still. Nothing to indicate the shocking violence which had taken place.

Black made his way out, and halfway to his car, he called the police. Perhaps something he should have done three hours earlier. He felt sudden despondency. Death followed him. He was the last person Penny Sinclair saw, before oblivion. A stranger. The despondency turned to shame. She had died not knowing why. Not with her mother or father. Not with anyone she loved or cared about.

He got to his car. There was a chill in the air. Or perhaps it was the chill in his bones. The sun was low, casting a wistful hue. There were few people about. Term time had finished, he surmised, and without the clamour and energy of young men and women, the place seemed bleak and sombre.

Penny Sinclair had been killed. Her life held no consequence to those such as Malcolm Copeland. Her death was a casual act of violence. She was training to be a lawyer, had worked in her father's firm. Probably doing little more than filing. Perhaps looking up obscure points of law. But to the mind of Malcolm Copeland, she was a link to his connection with her father. Thus, she had to die. Black saw the logic. But it was the logic of a monster.

Black pulled away, leaving Aberdeen University behind him.

Monsters were there to be killed.

That, to Black, was the perfect logic.

24

Deborah Gallagher knew that drink wasn't the answer, but it helped. Her husband had left the house for a jog on a mild summer's evening, and he never came home. Those last moments were branded into her mind, with searing clarity. His tattered training shoes, his Nike top, his running shorts. What he'd said. What she'd said in reply. He hadn't smiled as he left, and maybe that was the worst of it. Something was troubling him. But she hadn't pushed. He'd left, his heart heavy. And within half an hour, he was dead. No embrace goodbye. No tender words. No final farewell.

Death, when it came, held little regard for pleasantries.

But the drink helped. It softened the rough edges. It blurred the pain. It ushered away the nightmares to a shadowy corner of her mind. She was drinking two bottles of wine a day. At least. She still had to sort out her husband's affairs. She'd tried to contact her husband's partner, Charley Sinclair, but he wasn't picking up his mobile. She'd tried to phone the office, but it was closed. She had bills to pay. She worked part time in childcare, but the money she got wouldn't pay the mortgage or the electric or any god-damned fucking thing, except the wine.

It was six in the evening. She was sitting in the kitchen, alone. Her older son – Chris – had gone back to his barracks. Her other son, Tony, twelve, had descended into deep despondency. Before, he had been quiet, bordering on shy. Since the murder of his father, he rarely left his bedroom. He hadn't returned to school, and the authorities, whilst understanding the situation, wanted him back. She had a letter from the headmaster somewhere, suggesting strongly it was in his interests to return. Failing which, further action.

Fuck further action. Fuck them all.

On the breakfast bar was a bottle of cheap red wine, and a wine glass. She filled it up, took a drink. It tasted vile. A shade above vinegar. She began to sob. In sudden rage, she grabbed the bottle, flung it across the room. It hit the white tiled wall, a burst of glass and crimson. She couldn't live like this. Nor could Tony. *Pick yourself up. Be strong.* She thought of Adam Black. He'd lost his wife and daughter, murdered also. How the hell could anyone get over something like that. But he had. He told her she'd get through it. And for him, it wasn't some abstract notion. He spoke as one who knew, first hand.

She stood up, wobbled slightly, found her balance. She had more or less ignored Tony, suffused in her own self-pity. No more. She had to be strong, for both of them. For him. She went out of the kitchen, went upstairs. Tony's bedroom door was closed. She knocked on it, gently.

"Tony."

From within, silence.

She knocked again. "Tony."

Nothing. She opened the door. The curtains were closed. The room was in darkness. She made out his shape, in bed, under the covers. There was stuff strewn on the floor. Clothes, shoes, books. Unlike his older brother, Tony seemed to keep his room in perpetual chaos. Before, a constant irritation to

Deborah. Now, she loved him even more for it. She picked her way over to the window, opened the curtains, allowing in the early evening light. She made her way to the bed, knelt. She put her hand on the duvet.

"Tony," she whispered. She pulled back the cover.

And her world caved in.

25

A warrior lives by acting, not by thinking about acting, nor by thinking about what he will think when he has finished acting
— Carlos Castaneda

Black had two dead men in the boot of his car. It was a matter to be dealt with expeditiously. He drove to the Eaglesham Moors, a large area of tightly packed forest and tracts of wild grass and gorse. Black knew it well, having once lived only a couple of miles down the road in the village of Eaglesham.

He had run its myriad of paths many times. Some paths were well trodden. Others were secret. It was a secret path he chose that evening. He arrived at 10pm, taking a single lane road used for access for forestry traffic, and driving three miles, the trees thick on either side. He pulled into a grass verge. With no street lights, the dark was complete. There was hardly a sound. Black knew the way well enough. He had a torch, and found a narrow opening in the trees. He popped open the boot. Both bodies were cocooned in the travelling rugs. *Like pigs in blankets*, thought Black. He lifted one out, carried it fifty yards into the trees, repeated the process.

He rolled out the bodies of Daniel and Mr Neville. He left them where they lay. He retrieved the rugs, which he would burn later. The bodies would be found, in due course. Maybe weeks. Maybe months. Decomposition, and the wildlife, would render them unrecognisable. Black left, drove back to his flat in the south of Glasgow, then changed his mind, and went to a cheap hotel in the city. It was entirely conceivable Copeland would have Black's flat watched. On his way there, he stopped at an off sales, and bought a bottle of Glenfiddich.

The hotel was called the RedBrae Arms. A long flat-roofed structure, the stucco walls pale cream, and peeling. An altogether uninspiring building. At one end, a pub, which was quiet. Three television screens on the walls showed European football games. The place was drab and tired, but the prices were cheap. Black was unperturbed by the décor. His room was basic – a single bed, a small en suite.

Black had killed four of Copeland's men. Five, including Tristan, though that had been unintended. Copeland wouldn't let this go. Neither, for that matter, would Black. Black had an address, given to him by Daniel. Plus, he had two handguns. A helpful advantage. Black unscrewed the whisky bottle, took a slug. To Black's mind, the flavour never diminished. At times like this, when the world seemed bleak, if anything, the flavour got better.

"Fuck it," he muttered. Copeland would regroup, consider his options, plot Black's demise. Black couldn't allow this.

He screwed the top back on, placed the bottle on a bedside table.

Whisky would come later. Black had to act.

Now.

26

Another meeting was requested. Bustan was surprised at this. Normally, he only ever met people from the Remus Syndicate when cash was being delivered. Beyond that, instructions were given via mobile phone. A meeting therefore was unexpected, and Bustan didn't like the unexpected. A departure from the norm, in Bustan's world, meant trouble.

As such, he had to prepare. It occurred to him that perhaps they thought he had outlived his usefulness, and the meeting was a ruse, set up for his assassination. But he could be wrong, and if he refused, potentially, his cash cow might vanish, which was inconceivable for Bustan.

Greed always won. Bustan agreed to meet. At his shithole of a café. Bustan insisted. At least, if things went bad, he was on home turf.

A time was decided. Midnight. When the place was quiet. Bustan was there, occupying his usual table. Also, his fat friend, Yousef Kaya, who had stationed himself behind the counter under which, on a shelf, was a shotgun. Loaded. Sitting at his side, his nephew. Wire-thin narrow-pointed head shaved to the bone, restless button black eyes. Tucked in his belt, a Glock.

Four others, friends and distant cousins, all part of the Haytham Bustan mini empire, lured over from Turkey by easy money – to be made by a little violence, a little killing. Commonplace for such men, matters in which they were competent. Bustan was unaware what weapons they carried, but was confident they had ample fire power.

All the men were smoking. Plumes of tobacco coiled around them, dense and rich. The metal grills were down, both at the front window, and the front door. No light peeped through. From the outside, the place looked closed.

Bustan waited. He was anxious. He had no idea why he had been asked to meet. But they would know he would be prepared, and as such, he assumed killing wasn't on the agenda. Which meant they had a job for him. Which meant money.

At precisely midnight, there was a sharp rap on the front grill. Bustan nodded at Kaya, who lumbered over, grabbed the bottom of the shutters, hauled them up. A man stood at the entrance. Medium height, jeans, dark leather jacket, nondescript features. Looped over his shoulder, a duffel bag. Kaya stepped to one side. The man entered.

Kaya rolled the shutters down behind him. The man made his way directly to the table where Bustan sat. He placed the duffel bag on the tabletop. With care, signifying he was no danger, he pulled out a mobile phone from his jeans pocket, tapped the keypad, placed it beside the duffel bag.

A voice spoke on loudspeaker, disguised.

"There's fifty thousand in the bag."

Bustan nodded sagely, as if he were expecting just such a statement.

"A gift?"

"Not quite. More a payment to account. Fifty now, fifty upon completion."

"Ah. You require a service."

"One which you and your men are particularly good at. My colleague will provide you with two names and their addresses. It has to look good. You understand, I'm sure. A random hit-and-run. A burglary gone wrong. Whatever seems appropriate. Nothing to suggest they were targeted. However you do it, the conclusion has to be… final."

"Final. I understand."

"The second fifty you'll get when the task is completed. Do you accept?"

Bustan inhaled deeply, flicked the cigarette on a saucer improvising as an ashtray. It was already full. *Do you accept?* Of course he did. He was being asked to fulfil a task which, for him and his men, was as routine as ordering lunch.

"Yes."

The man standing before him reached into his inside jacket pocket, took out an envelope, dropped it on the table. He picked up the phone, turned, and left the café, the fat man, Kaya, opening and closing the shutters.

Bustan drew a deep sigh. Soon – maybe a year, maybe two – he would retire to his villa by the sea. Sit on the beach, listen to the sound of the surf. One part of his mind scoffed at such a notion. Bustan loved money too much to ever give up. That part of his mind said – *you'll never leave this game. As long as the cash rolls in, the killing will never stop.*

And easy money was the best money.

The man sitting beside him – his nephew – pulled open the duffel bag, and started fishing the money out. Rolls of fifties and twenties. He would count it, because it would have been imprudent not to. But Bustan knew the people who paid him were never inaccurate when it came to money. Of more interest were the contents of the envelope.

He stubbed his cigarette on the saucer, and immediately lit

up another one. Another deep inhalation, exhaling smoke through his nose. He opened the envelope.

Two names, printed.

Charles Sinclair.

Deborah Gallagher.

Two people who had no idea of the fate awaiting them. Just bad luck. But good luck for him. He would plan their deaths, and do it quickly.

Jason Drummond disconnected. The Turks were talented at the job they'd been given. Plus, they were expendable. If things went to fuck, then they were easy to blame. But he knew the manner of the man, Bustan, and knew Bustan loved his money too much to allow failure.

Drummond sat back in his office, pondered. People imagined that for things like this, money would be wire transferred, discreetly handled, from one anonymous bank account to another. But Drummond knew people, and people liked the touch and smell of cash. Handed over in a safe place in something as simple as a briefcase, sports holdall or a plastic bag. Create all the technology you wanted, for things like this, cash was still king.

And Drummond knew when he offered a man like Bustan hard cash, then such a man would dance to any damned tune he played.

27

Daniel, minutes before his death, had provided Black with Malcolm Copeland's address. Two miles outside the town of Biggar. A country mansion. A fortress, more like. Copeland may not be there. If he was, Black had to assume he would have ramped up his security. Copeland's priority was the destruction of Adam Black. Black therefore had to turn the tables.

The Special Air Service were experts in the unorthodox. Surprise, confuse, disorientate. Hunting in small packs allowed greater mobility – to strike hard and fast, then vanish in the shadows, only to reappear at times and places the enemy could not predict. And each time they struck, a little piece of the enemy's morale was chipped away.

Surprise, confuse, disorientate. Think like the enemy, then do what they least expected. The more audacious the better. Sometimes, the simplest plan was the best. Simple and direct, and probably the last thing Malcolm Copeland would anticipate.

It was after midnight. Clouds hid the moon and the stars, heightening the gloom. The journey from Glasgow to Biggar took an hour and a half. Daniel's information had been precise. Black used the satnav in his car, and established the location of Copeland's house without difficulty. Millard House. Blackwater Reservoir. The roads, at that time, were quiet. Black had a collection of four pistols. Those once owned by Daniel and Mr Neville, and those belonging to the two men Black had confronted in Penny Sinclair's room. Specifically, two Berettas, and two Glocks.

He reached the town of Biggar. It was a quiet, picture postcard place, the main street quaint and rural, houses fronting directly onto the pavement, built of old solid stone, doors and windows colourful with black and beige trim. High-peaked slate roofs, crow stepped gables. A small common green, in the centre of which, clustered round magnolia trees, a white marble war memorial.

He had checked the internet. There were five hotels. He'd booked a room in the Elphinstone Manor, for two nights. He'd explained to the receptionist that he would be arriving late. *No problem*, was the reply. *We're open through the night, and you can pick up the keys at the front counter. Hope you enjoy your visit.* Black paid by card, and said he was sure he would. On his way there, he stopped off at a twenty-four-hour superstore, and purchased a specific item.

Black found the hotel easily enough. On a side road, off the main street. An unassuming Victorian mid-terraced building of coloured sandstone, and arched bevelled windows, providing, at least from the front, an *olde worlde* feel. He slowed down. The road was not wide, and one-way. A single car was parked opposite, half on the pavement. In it, the driver, his head a shadowy silhouette.

Black allowed himself a half smile. He reckoned his hunch had paid off – *think like the enemy.* Copeland would make damned sure there were no surprises. He would undoubtedly beef up the security round his house. But he'd go that extra mile, for sure. Have men watch the hotels in the town, to look out for strangers coming in. Black might be wrong, of course. But it was a logical plan of action for a man fearful for his life, and with money and resource. Plus, thought Black grimly, it was what he would do.

Think like the enemy.

Black drove by. Google Maps had told him there was a car park a hundred and fifty yards from the hotel entrance. He pulled in, parked, got out. He made his way back, towards the car, in an almost nonchalant manner. Too fast would arouse suspicion, and suggest crisis. He approached the car, raised a hand. The driver watched him, perplexed, slid his window down three inches. Black leaned forward.

"We've found him," he said. "Copeland's told us to come back in."

The driver – a lean-faced man, white hair cut short and square across his forehead, small pebble-black eyes – scrutinised him for several seconds. "Where did they find him?"

Black put a hand to his ear, shook his head. "What?"

The driver lowered his window fully down. "Where did they..."

He never finished the sentence. Black moved, a short vicious strike, thrusting maximum impact into the driver's thorax, crushing the windpipe. His head snapped back. He released a short rattling gasp. Black followed up with two crunching punches, targeting nose and chin, possibly breaking both. The driver slumped across onto the passenger's seat.

Casually, Black reached in. The car was a BMW 5-series, press button ignition. The keys were in the central console compartment. Black lifted them out, put them in his jacket pocket. The driver was out cold. Might even be dead. Black hardly cared. He made his way to his own car, popped open the boot. The same space where, only two hours before, he'd bundled two rolled-up rugs containing the corpses of Daniel and Mr Neville. He retrieved his sports bag.

He returned to the hotel, entered. The place was surprisingly elegant, belying its somewhat unassuming exterior. High ceilings, the reception area dark-wood panelling, glowing a soft rosy hue from discreet downlighters. The front desk was brass and shot marble. A young woman sat behind, typing on a keyboard, gazing at a computer screen. Her face became instantly animated when she saw Black.

"Yes, sir?"

"I booked a room earlier. Sorry for the lateness of the hour. The name's Black. Adam Black."

"Of course." She was young and pretty. Wearing a pale blue uniform. Pinned to her shoulder, a silver name badge – *Louise*. She gazed at the screen, fingers clicking.

"Yes, Mr Black. I have you here. Two nights?"

"Yes."

She nodded, smiling. She put a door entry card on the marble top. "Breakfast's between 6.45 and 9.30. Your room is on the first floor. The lift is to the left. I hope you enjoy your stay, Mr Black."

"Thank you, Louise. I'm sure I will. I'll take the stairs."

"Of course."

Black made his way up a set of broad carpeted stairs, got to the first floor. He had chosen it specifically. He found his room, entered, placed the entry card into a slot. Light flickered on. The room was of regular dimensions, clean, comprising the basic requirements. Bed, fitted wardrobes, a TV, an en suite. In a corner, a chair and a writing desk, upon which, a kettle, a plate of complimentary shortbread, and a tray of tea, coffee and sugar sachets with miniature milk cartons.

Beside the writing desk, a window. Double glazed, tilt and

turn. The view was unspectacular – the side of a red-brick building, windowless, separated from the hotel by a narrow lane, given weak illumination from a single sconce attached to the bricks.

Black opened the bedroom window, looked down. A drop of maybe over twenty feet. If he jumped, he'd break his legs, and possibly his neck. Black had no such intention. He opened the sports bag, put the two Berettas in his jacket pockets, tucked a Glock under his trouser belt. The shotgun was too awkward. He retrieved the item he'd bought at the superstore – a coil of rope from the outdoor section. He tied one end round a leg of the bed, let it fall into the lane below. He removed the door entry card. The room was sudden darkness.

Black manoeuvred himself out the window, let the rope take his weight, and lowered himself to the ground. He left the rope, hoping it wouldn't be spotted. Unlikely, in the darkness. Still, it was down to luck. Perhaps tonight, his luck might run out. And then? Black didn't care to finish the thought.

He walked the length of the lane, to the main road, hugging the shadows. There, opposite the hotel, a matter of thirty yards or so, the BMW, remaining as before. He sauntered across the road, to the driver's door, opened it. The driver hadn't moved.

Black bundled him across, manoeuvring legs and arms, until he had him sitting up in the passenger seat. His head lolled forward, chin resting on his collarbone. At first glance, he could have been sleeping. Black sat in the driver's seat, reached over, unbuttoned the man's jacket, revealing a shoulder holster, complete with a snub-nose Ruger revolver. Compact and powerful. Black removed it, tucked it in an inside pocket. He checked the glove compartment.

Inside, a Desert Eagle, together with silencer. Powerful enough to knock a man's head from his shoulders. Clearly, Copeland wasn't underestimating the situation. Black placed it in a side compartment of the driver's door. He started the car. The engine hummed into life. He put Copeland's address in the satnav, turned the voice to mute, and pulled off. The destination was approximately two miles, and would take all of five minutes.

Black kept the speed low. He needed luck more than ever. He was basing everything on a hunch. *Think like the enemy.* Black assumed Copeland would fortify his position. He wouldn't expect a direct attack by Black, but it wouldn't do any harm to beef up security. He had the money. Therefore, why not? He would hire external help. Possibly an outside, bespoke, quasi-legal security firm. Maybe even two. Firms who would perform a little wet work, for the right price.

Possibly another twenty men, over and above Copeland's existing team. Which meant new faces, and thus a fundamental flaw – recognition became complicated. If conditions were right, assumptions were made. Wrong assumptions. Allowing Black to exploit.

Or so he hoped. If it went wrong, and he got captured, then the game was over, and he would die. Some game, yet it was the only game Black played, because it was the only game he enjoyed.

28

The Remus Syndicate had given Bustan two names and addresses. Charles Sinclair and Deborah Gallagher. Two assassinations. This, for Bustan, was easy work. In the backstreets of Istanbul, killing was simple. And he had a knack for it. He'd started in his teens, and realised quickly, to make your way in the world from a dirt-poor beginning, it was easier to kill the competition than outsmart them. Things changed, as he got older. He was head of his own gang. His own *family*. Others did his bidding. He commanded, they performed. And willingly, to get praise and kudos. And money, of course.

Money laundering, extortion, people trafficking. To name just a few. His empire had all started with killing, and his willingness to do it, and do it well. Thus, when he was tasked to kill two strangers, his reaction was almost instinctive. Easy work, easy money. He didn't miss a beat when he accepted.

The jobs were to be done on consecutive nights, each executed by a different team. The first kill was Charles Sinclair. Bustan had instructed his nephew to complete the task – a man in his early thirties called Altan – along with three others. No pistols. Clubs and hammers. It was to look like a burglary. Most burglars didn't go armed with semi-automatics.

They got to his house in Strathaven in the early hours, parked a hundred yards away in a stolen white van, jogged to the house. They crept round the back, four shadows, and jemmied the rear French doors, which were easy to open. They expected an alarm. An alarm only meant they had a little less time to fulfil their task. Experience told them it had little practical effect other than scaring away the hesitant thief. But for the committed criminal, an alarm was a mere annoyance. It woke the owner, sure. But intimidation, maybe a little violence, kept them quiet. As for neighbours, an alarm was usually ignored, treated as an irritation. If hardwired direct to the police, the cavalry didn't generally arrive for a full half-hour. Plenty of time for fun and games.

But there was no alarm. All was quiet. They made their way in, through the kitchen, got to the hallway, where they stopped, stunned into sudden freeze mode.

It was then that Altan made the call to his uncle.

"He's dead," he said, his voice a whisper.

Bustan delayed his response, as he considered the two words his nephew had just uttered.

"How?"

"He's hanging. Looks like a cord round the neck. In the hall."

Another pause, then – "You'd better make sure. Cut him down. Then use the clubs. Leave your mark."

Bustan disconnected. He couldn't have cared less about Charley Sinclair and his apparent suicide. What he did care about was not getting paid. He didn't want any loopholes in his arrangement. The deal was simple. He got paid once he'd arrange his death. The Syndicate could argue that Sinclair was already dead, and thus renege. Better therefore to be sure, and smash the man's head to a pulp.

Just to be sure.

29

Malcolm Copeland had indeed ramped up his security, as Black had predicted. Those close to him – *his inner sanctum* – comprised twelve men who had worked with him for over twenty years. Men who were eminently capable, and loyal. And who committed acts of violence without compunction. Copeland had contracted in another twenty-five men from a security firm based in London, at a cost of £21,000 per man, for a period of one week.

The cost was an irrelevance. If he needed them for longer, then he would pay whatever was asked, until he had Black's liver pinned to his front door. He had stationed a man at each hotel in the surrounding area. He had a man at the front electric gates, plus five men patrolling the grounds, with Dobermans. He had four sentries at the front, four at the back, at various locations. The rest were inside, moving room to room, circulating. Essentially, he had a small army at his disposal. He was, to his mind, untouchable.

He'd shipped his wife and kids out to a house they had deep in the Lake District. She hadn't objected. She accepted the downside to their lives with a quiet, grim resignation. The houses, the pool, the private education, the money, the clothes – she never asked where it all came from, because she didn't dare. She'd sold her soul to the devil, and knew the consequences. Better then to accept, because there was nothing else she could do. She therefore chose never to ask questions, too fearful of what the answers might be.

Copeland stayed in the main living room – the same room where Daniel had explained about the man called Adam Black. The lights were muted. It was a summer's night, yet Copeland had insisted on having a real fire crackling, for no other reason than he found it therapeutic.

He sat at one end of an Italian leather couch, cradling a glass of Bombay Sapphire Gin with tonic. On the armrest, an ashtray, upon which rested a lit cigar. Smoke weaved through in the air, the room suffused with its heavy scent. In the half light, furniture was reduced to shapes and shadows. Outside, at the French windows, a silhouette – a watchful guard. Another man entered the room. Dressed in a neat suit, opened-necked shirt, muscular, economical of motion.

"You all right, Mr Copeland?"

Copeland looked up. He didn't recognise him. One of the new guys. He nodded. The man nodded back, did a quick check of the room, left.

Copeland took a drink. He preferred whisky, but it gave him heartburn. Acid reflux, as described by one of his doctors. Keep drinking, the doctors had said, and the acid will burn a hole in your oesophagus. Fuck the doctors. He lifted the cigar to his lips, sucked in the tobacco. Feeling the bite in his lungs. He replaced it back on the ashtray – a porcelain saucer he'd got from the kitchen. He pondered.

What would he do if he were Black? Run. Probably. All Copeland's enemies either ran or died. Few, if any, resisted.

Malcolm Copeland was feared. His name was his brand. You don't dare fuck with Malcolm Copeland.

But the fundamental problem was that Black had done exactly that. He'd popped up out of nowhere, like a demon in the night, and within the space of a few short days, had killed Tristan, Daniel, Neville, and two others in Aberdeen. Five men. Copeland took a deep breath, tinged with a slight wheeze. Black had started it. Copeland's men had visited Charley Sinclair, and Black had retaliated. In Copeland's world, retaliation, no matter how slight, required a swift and brutal response. What did Black expect? But Black had responded right back, like a fury.

Copeland juggled the question in his mind. *What would Black do?* Copeland adjusted his thoughts. Black was no runner. He didn't flee from danger. The opposite. He embraced it. And he was no stranger to the game. Copeland couldn't afford to give this up. If he let Black go, what next? What other enemies would come crawling out from beneath the rocks. Black knew this. Black's need to end this was as powerful as Copeland's.

Black would come. Copeland felt it in his blood, his soul.

Good, then. Let it play. Let the scrapper come. He took another swig of the gin, let its strong bitter liquid slide down his throat.

And yet... He licked his lips, placed the glass on the armrest of the couch, sat back, stared at the crackling flames in the hearth, watching them spark and flicker.

He felt something he hadn't experienced for many years. A flutter deep in his chest; a cold whisper in his mind.

An emotion he thought he was immune from.

Fear.

30

The man in the passenger seat groaned, wobbled his head. Black was about a mile outside Biggar, on a country road, devoid of any street lighting. The night sky was clear and cloudless. On either side, a landscape of darkness, the fields and trees tinged with the silver reflection of the moon. He pulled over, onto a grass verge. Black reached across, positioned his arms round the man's neck, creating a lock, made a short sharp movement. The neck snapped. Black unfastened the man's seat belt, relieved him of his wallet, and rolled him out of the car.

Black checked the contents. The deceased was called Harry James. Driver's licence, some credit cards, two hundred pounds in crisp twenties, a gym pass, a golf club membership card.

"Can't see your handicap improving, Harry."

Black drove off. According to the satnav, Copeland's house was close. He kept his speed low. To his left, another road, easily missed in the darkness. This, according to the map, was his route. He turned, reducing his speed further. The road was narrow, barely wide enough for one car, the surface bumpy and uneven. Trees loomed on either side, forming almost an archway, moonlight glinting through the branches. A quarter of a mile.

Black's mind prickled with imminence. He was approaching the monster's lair. His plan was simple and direct. Uncomplicated. Its success was based on Copeland overcompensating. Of course, Copeland might not be there. He might have hidden himself away, in another location, another country. But Black thought not. Men like Copeland had to show face. When it got down to brass tacks, Copeland was nothing more than a gang leader. And if leaders ran away, then reputation – respect – vanished. And men like Copeland survived on their reputation.

The road followed a long curve. Destination three hundred yards. The trees disappeared suddenly. Ahead, double gates, illuminated by sconces set on stone pillars, and on either side, six feet high walls, stretching into the gloom. At the gates, a dark shape. A guard. Black's senses sharpened to a higher level of competence.

Fear, when it came to Black, came strangely. He was able to compartmentalise it. Package it, contain it, and then, in an almost out-of-body experience, consider events from a distance. Now was such a moment. He saw himself drive towards the gates. He saw himself slowing the car, one hand on the steering wheel, one hand on his lap, manner relaxed. At his side, in the door compartment, rested the Desert Eagle.

He stopped at the gates. The man was dressed in dark trousers, dark tunic. Thickset shoulders, lean hips and waist. Dark hair cropped short. Face as emotionless as a rock. He held an Armalite AR-10 Semi-Automatic rifle, and looked like a man who knew how to use it. He checked the licence plate on the car, checked his mobile phone. He tapped Black's window. Black pressed a button. The window eased down.

Black waited. He had one hand wrapped round the Desert

Eagle, at his side. It was 50/50. Two seconds for the man to straighten the rifle, point. Two seconds for Black to raise the pistol, point.

The man scrutinised Black.

"Why are you back?" he said.

Black responded, keeping his voice neutral.

"Don't know. Mr Copeland wanted to speak to me. Nothing happening here?"

The man twitched his head in the negative. "All quiet. Park the car round the back."

"No problem."

The man spoke into his mobile, relaying the licence number. A pause. Then the gates rumbled open. Black drove through. His hunch appeared to have played out – Copeland had hired an abundance of men. The guard had only checked the licence number of the car. If it matched, the box was ticked. It was relatively simple for Black to exploit the situation, slipping through disorganisation.

Black drove the BMW all of a hundred yards, along a paved driveway. On either side, a low rough stone wall with lights at regular intervals, and beyond, flat manicured lawns. Ahead, a substantial mansion, illuminated by bright uplighters, red ivy glistening on the lower walls. Three levels, plus attic dormers. At one end, a turret, with glittering stained-glass windows. On the top floor, balconies of gothic wrought iron mounted on stone supports.

The main entrance was pillared, with arched wooden doors, about which congregated several men. Black saw other men walking across the lawns. He passed them, driving round the side, to the rear, to the back garden area. More lighting, but here, the gardens were mature, covering at least two acres in size, enclosed by more low stone walls, and on all sides, the brooding gloom of a thick forest.

Black parked the car next to others. More men hovered. Two stood at the rear entrance. At one end, a large conservatory. Black took a deep calming breath. So far, so good. It could end in a second. Someone might click, questioning Black. And then? Black had a measure of reassurance, by way of the two Berettas and the awesome firing power of the Desert Eagle. The Berettas he kept in his trouser pockets. The Desert Eagle, with the silencer, he tucked under his belt, and kept the front of his jacket fastened.

He approached the back entrance. A man stepped forward. About the same height as Black – six two. Long rangy arms, thick shoulders. Face all bone and sharp edges. He stared at Black with an unnerving intensity. In his hand, he held a mobile phone.

"Name," he said, in a strong London accent.

"Harry James."

The man used his finger to slide down the screen of his mobile. He grunted, twitched his head.

"Okay. Why are you back? You should be at the hotel."

"Mr Copeland wants to see me."

"Jesus," the man muttered. "The last to know, as usual. What does he want?"

Black raised his hands, feigning bewilderment. "Listen, I don't make the rules. I'm told to come, I come. Who knows why?"

The man nodded with sympathy. "I get it. It's a fucking circus. Okay, Harry. He's in the big lounge."

"Yes?"

"Through the kitchen. Turn left, the room at the end of the hall. The size of this fucking place, you need a pair of hiking boots." He gave a wide grin. "You like that?"

"You should be doing stand-up."

Black entered the house of Malcolm Copeland. So far, so

good. He'd been lucky. His gamble had paid off. Would his luck hold? Probably not, he thought with a grim resignation. Chance was, he'd end up dead. A bullet in the head. Probably more than one. Then his body dumped in a hole deep in the ground, in a nameless patch of Scottish wilderness. And thus the end of Adam Black.

But Black didn't care. Death did not frighten him. Indeed, he welcomed it. More than welcome. It was, if he were honest with himself, a desire. A craving. But he craved something else. Justice.

Justice for an innocent girl he had met only once, in her dying breath. Justice for Penny Sinclair.

31

Bustan's plan was to arrange the killing of Deborah Gallagher the following evening. Also, on the same evening, the next batch was due to arrive at Bustan's tenement flat in the south side. Captain Abasolo would deposit them – specifically, a family of six comprising mother, father, and four kids – at a location on the Cornish coast in about two hours.

To Bustan's mind, this aspect of the schedule was always the most precarious. The Coast Guard, and the Navy, were diligent. Avoiding them was difficult, almost an art. But Abasolo was cunning. He'd run the trafficking game for many years, during which, he'd never been caught. *There was always a first.* To augment the difficulty, right-wing self-appointed migrant hunters scoured the coastline, vigilant and violent.

It was past midnight. Bustan lived in an unassuming house in an area of Glasgow called Kingspark, amongst hundreds of similar buildings. He kept his garden neat, his windows clean. He was always quiet. One car at the most parked in the driveway. Nothing to draw attention to himself. Boundary fences not too high, not too low.

He rented it from a company. If the company were dissected,

eventually, after much peeling away, one would discover he was the beneficial owner. The contents of the house were spartan. Nothing personal. No photographs, no family memorabilia, no personal effects, save some clothes in a wardrobe. Nothing to trace Bustan to anything. If Bustan had to leave suddenly, there was nothing there to suggest he existed.

He was watching a movie on television in the living room. A Hollywood blockbuster. In the same room were two of his men. Distant relations. Half cousins, or something of the sort. Bustan lost track. They could barely speak a word of English. Bustan wondered why the hell they were so engrossed in a movie with English dialogue. They were sitting round a coffee table. On it, an ashtray, a large bowl of crisps, and his mobile phone.

It suddenly vibrated on the wooden tabletop. Bustan stretched over, picked it up. It was Captain Abasolo. No problems. He was on schedule. A family of six. The kids were tired, but quietly excited. The parents anxious. He'd drop anchor three hundred yards off the appointed rendezvous – Polridmouth Cove. Then, with a calm sea, an easy dinghy row to a secluded shoreline, where two cars would meet them, for the long journey north, to one of Bustan's little flats in Govanhill, where he greeted all the new faces, and promised them paradise.

This time however, modifications were required. The instructions given to him were specific. Children only. He had to choreograph events to cause minimum alarm. He would arrange for the children to travel in one car to the hospital, explain to the parents they had to go separately. He would come up with some bullshit story. When it came to bullshit, Bustan was an expert. The parents would never leave. At least not alive.

Bustan came to a decision. He'd slit their throats in the flat. Or maybe strangle them. Not him personally, of course. Others would do that. Bustan pondered. His old friend, Yousef Kaya, performed such tasks with efficiency and skill. To a man like Kaya, killing another human being was like killing an animal. Plus, he was proficient at butchering. He would dismember the bodies with precision, and pack them away in an orderly manner. *Yes, Kaya's the man.*

Bustan put the mobile phone back on the table, got some crisps from the bowl, and turned his attention back to the movie. Unlike his relatives, he understood the dialogue perfectly.

32

Black made his way along the corridor. It was wide and high, the walls dark marble shot with silver flecks, the ceiling a series of gilt-edged cupolas, from which suspended miniature chandeliers, sparkling like little clouds of stars. Doors on either side. Black passed two men in the corridor, who gave him a cursory glance. Black walked like a man who belonged. Part of the Malcolm Copeland protection team. He reached a leather panelled door at the end, turned the handle, pushed.

He entered a large dimly lit room. All about, shapes and shadows. At one end, a fire crackled under a stone hearth. Above it, an enormous painting of a man dressed from another era, sporting a shotgun. The same man was sitting on a couch close to the fire, only considerably fatter. He was swaddled in a crimson silk bathrobe. On his feet a pair of matching slippers. Clasped in one hand, a glass of something probably alcoholic. Burning on an ashtray on the arm of the couch, a cigar. The man himself, presumed Black. Malcolm Copeland.

Copeland barely looked at him. He seemed absorbed in the flickering flames of the fire. Black noted the far wall, comprising a set of French doors, beyond which, a man stood as motionless as stone, his back to the room, looking out towards the gardens. Watching for any advancing intruders. Oblivious to the intruder within. As indeed everyone was.

"What is it," growled Copeland. He picked up his cigar, sucked at one end, the other turning a sudden glowing circle of orange.

Black remained at the door. He spoke, soft as a breath. "Do you have a minute, Mr Copeland?"

"What?" Copeland looked up, peering at him.

Black made his way in, a shadow amongst shadows, and stood before the fire, six feet from Copeland.

"Just a minute of your time, please. It won't take long, I promise." Black sat on a chair opposite. Copeland's face contorted in bewilderment.

"What is this? You should be out there, doing what you're fucking paid to do."

"Of course. I couldn't agree more. But this will only take a moment. I have something important to tell you."

Copeland squinted. "It had better be important. Come closer, so I can see your face."

"Hush now," said Black. "Adam Black is near at hand."

Copeland jerked up, the contents of the glass spilling on his lap, his robe slipping to one side, revealing a patch of smooth skin, white as alabaster. The jowls of his face quivered, like a slobbery dog.

"What do you mean, *near at hand*? Who are you?"

"Adam Black is here."

With an almost casual air, Black produced the Desert Eagle, and aimed it at Copeland's midsection. It was an easy target.

"You'll know your weapons, I'm sure. This particular handgun is particularly powerful. Do you know why? Let me tell you. It has a gas-operated chamber. That's unique for a semi-automatic. As such, it can take cartridges that pack a real punch. For example, if I were to aim for your neck…" Black tilted the pistol up four inches, "…the impact would remove your head from your shoulders. If I aimed for your stomach, not only would the bullet shred your internal organs, but it would keep going, like it was on a holiday, and rip through the back of the couch, and through the French doors, and cut the guy outside in half. I would describe this a mean motherfucker of a gun. Yes?"

Sweat dribbled from every pore of Copeland's bald head, down into his eyes. He blinked, licked his lips with a small darting pink tongue. He cleared his throat, tried to speak, but managed only a dry rattle. He swallowed, tried again, and found his voice.

"You've got a set of balls. Coming in here. Doing what you're doing. Shoot me, and you'll last ten seconds. For what?"

Black said nothing.

Copeland continued, voice a harsh rasp. "For what? We both die. Fuck it. Maybe we could both live. Maybe we could turn this to our advantage."

Black said nothing.

Copeland's tone, perhaps thinking Black's lack of response was a form of tacit interest, became more confident.

"I've got over thirty guys out and about. Yet you still got through. I could use a man like you. You could name your price. Win fucking win, for both of us." He glanced round, to the guard outside.

"He's not going to help you," Black said. "Work for you? What would you have me do? Kill innocents? You arranged for two men to kill a young girl you'd never met. Is that the type of work you'd have me do? Is that the type of man you think I am?"

Copeland swallowed again. He took a large wheezing breath, then another. "It's the way it is."

"And Desmond Gallagher. He found out you were

laundering money and so you raised one of your fat fingers and ordered his death."

Copeland shook his head. "Gallagher? The lawyer? That wasn't me. I never did that. Listen to me, Black, let's be reasonable about this."

"Let's." Black straightened his arm, cocked his head as if considering his target, pointed the pistol at Copeland's chest. Copeland raised his arm. He gasped, managing an inarticulate mumble. Suddenly he straightened, arching his spine, clutching his chest. His face went tight, his skin bone-white and slick with sweat. His breathing came in a great heaving shudder. He convulsed, arched further forward, started to spasm, glass and cigar knocked to the carpet. Outside, the guard remained unaware.

"Let me help," Black said. He got up, strode forward, grabbed a large embroidered cushion, pressed it down hard onto Copeland's face, mounted him, using his body weight to thrust Copeland back against the couch. Copeland jerked and twitched, both arms flapping in his silk gown like monstrous red wings. Black pushed harder. Copeland's movements lessened, became still. Black waited a little longer, removed the cushion. He stared into Copeland's face, slack and lifeless.

"Compliments of Penny Sinclair," he whispered. He picked up the fallen cigar, and pushed it into Copeland's mouth. He got the glass. A sliver of drink remained. Black sniffed, detecting the unmistakable aroma of gin. Waste not, want not, he thought, and downed the contents. He placed the glass in one of Copeland's pudgy hands, and gave Copeland's face a gentle slap.

"Enjoy your evening."

Black made his way out of the room, silent as a wraith, as if he'd never been.

He went out the same way as he had come, the men at the back door nodding as he left.

"Did you speak to the boss?" enquired the same guard Black had dialogued with upon his initial entrance.

"Yup. All good. Left him with his cigar and gin." *And a heart attack.* "Think he wants to be left alone a while. Better get back."

"Understood."

Black reached the BMW, bleeped the alarm, got in. Guards still roamed the rear gardens, oblivious their paymaster was a corpse. Black eased the car round the side, drove slowly along the main driveway. The man at the front gate waved at him, and the gates trundled open. Black drove the stretch of pot-marked lane, the car lurching and bouncing, until he got to the main road. He turned, made his way back to Biggar.

After a mile, he pulled in and steered across a grassy verge, down a slope and into a trough separating the road from a wood. He got out, and walked the mile back, keeping to the shadows. It would take a while before the car would be found.

He returned without incident. He could only assume no one had twigged Copeland was dead, otherwise he would have encountered a rushing ambulance. He reached his hotel, and made his way along the narrow side path below his window. There! The rope remained as before. He pulled himself up, and climbed into his bedroom, pulling the rope up behind him. His room was uncomfortably warm. He kept the window open.

A productive night. A measure of redress had been achieved, the scales balanced. Penny Sinclair had been murdered. Black had returned the compliment, and Copeland was dead. And he hoped, with his death, his crew would lose motivation and focus. After all, who would pay them?

And yet... Copeland had denied killing Desmond Gallagher. There was no reason for him to lie about such a thing.

The mystery of Gallagher's death remained, or so it seemed. Black thought back, to the funeral, to the conversation with

Gallagher's wife, and to the threats they had received, from an entity called the Remus Syndicate.

This wasn't over. Not by a country mile. Black lay on the bed, and fell asleep in his clothes.

33

Black woke early the next morning, showered, changed into dark jeans, a dark long-sleeved sports top, a pair of well-used running shoes. He went downstairs for breakfast at 7am, to a large ornate dining room, with wide bay windows overlooking a quaint, well-ordered garden. The food was laid out in rows of hot plates, buffet style. Black was famished. He heaped bacon, eggs, sausages on his plate. The place was empty, save for a young couple at one corner.

Black took a complimentary newspaper from a rack, sat nearest the windows. The skies were heavy with cloud. Looked like rain was coming. A waitress brought over a round of toast and a pot of coffee. He flicked through the paper. There was nothing of interest. He finished breakfast, poured himself a third cup of coffee, caught the waitress's attention, and asked for a fresh pot, and more toast. He sat back, gazing at the scenery outside, though there was little to see. It was a neat garden, high walls on either side, a patch of lawn, and in the centre, a cherry tree, dense with clustered double pink flowers. From a branch hung a lantern shaped bird feeder. On it was a solitary robin, fearless, picking at the morsels of seed.

Black, prone to bouts of melancholic introspection, thought back, to another time, another world. Memories came back. Once, in the Khogyani District of Afghanistan, near the border of Pakistan, he and a small team of handpicked Special Forces were on a reconnaissance sweep. Taliban were believed to have gone on a "revenge hunt". Door-to-door killings, seeking western collaborators in a number of villages. Black's job was to evaluate and return, not to intercede. Black got to a village called Zawa. There was little left. The houses burnt and pulverised. Body parts on the dirt tracks. Women, children, animals. Death didn't discriminate.

The smell of smoked flesh attacked the senses. No one was alive. The village, its population, reduced to memories. This was no Taliban strike. The carnage was too complete. Too perfect. This was a drone strike. Maybe the US. Maybe the British Army. Black didn't know, and would never know. A drone strike gone way off target. A frequent event, in the badlands of Afghanistan. The so-called "surgical accuracy" a myth. If the military got a whiff of Taliban activity, then the response was simple – kill, kill, kill.

He and his men picked their way through the devastation, silent and grim. He remembered – in the doorway of a broken house, beside the body of a little girl no older than four, a tiny bird. A robin redbreast. Bright amongst the ruins. Fearless. Black had never seen one in Afghanistan, but he saw one there, in that village, standing strong beside the child. Daring him to come closer. A guardian of the dead. A tiny splash of colour in the dark. It brought what? Black recalled the emotion. Something in that tragic world he thought never to see. Hope.

Black drew his thoughts to the present, and wondered how things were playing out. By now, almost certainly, Copeland's death was an established fact. The multitude of men he'd hired would be milling about, debating where their next pay cheque was coming from. In a short while, he reckoned, they would disband, return to whichever rock they'd crawled from.

Copeland's manner of death, in the first instance, wouldn't arouse suspicion. But in time, the BMW would be found, as well as the body of the unfortunate Harry James, his neck twisted at an ugly angle. Who would care? The police would think gangland killing, a frequent occurrence in the Malcolm Copeland universe. And retribution? Hardly. With Copeland gone, others would be too interested in filling his space, perhaps leading to warfare. Hopefully, the name Adam Black would fade into oblivion, like footprints in the sand.

The vibration of his mobile phone roused him from his thoughts. He reached into his pocket, glanced at the number. Deborah Gallagher. He answered. "Deborah?"

"Please come, Adam."

Black sensed the strain in her voice. "What is it?"

"My son. Tony. He..." Black heard her hesitate, take a long breath.

He waited.

"He tried to kill himself."

A short brutal statement. Black missed a beat, trying to rationalise. He spoke, and knew what he said wouldn't help one iota.

"I'm so sorry, Deborah."

"Please come. I'm at the house."

"Give me an hour."

Black disconnected, looked out into the hotel's back garden.

The robin had gone.

34

Doctors Michael Stapleton and Percy Canning never worked on the morning prior to the delivery of fresh intakes. Instead, they played squash. It had become almost a ritual. Nor were they members of a squash club. Stapleton lived in a baronial-style mansion in the Pentland Hills, twenty miles from Edinburgh. He'd paid over a million for it. Initially, an abandoned semi-derelict wreck, but to his mind, a bargain, with potential.

He'd spent another two million in upgrading. Built a new roof, eradicated the rot, strengthened walls, adding turrets, parapets and terraces. At the rear, he had built a squash court, constructed entirely of glass. It had its own exclusive bar with a small viewing balcony, plus showers, and a steam room. All bought and paid for, courtesy of the people brought to him every six weeks by the man called Bustan. In time, maybe a couple of years or so, he would sell, make a profit, and move on.

They played on those special mornings, early. Just the two of them. Best of five games. Stapleton was twenty-five years older, but won every time. Not that Canning was a poor player. Stapleton was better, and supremely fit. He'd played rugby as a young man, and as a matter of habit, had maintained a strict regime of fitness throughout his life.

He was sixty-six and still managed forty minutes on a treadmill each morning before his drive to the hospital. He walked miles every weekend, had climbed every Munro Scotland had to offer. He trained with light weights four times a week. He was lean and hard as wire. He got up at dawn, rarely went to bed after nine. He watched what he ate, and took care to exclude sugar and red meat from his diet. He'd never married. He liked the idea of spending his money exclusively on himself.

Every few weeks – six, in fact – Stapleton and Canning performed the ritual. Canning would stay the night, and in the morning, they played squash. This particular morning, nothing had changed. Stapleton had won again, and Canning, who really didn't give a shit, was graceful in defeat.

They were sitting at the bar, on the balcony overlooking the squash court. The vista beyond was tranquil. Low green hills, rising and falling like an ocean swell. In the distance, a patch of silver-blue – Harlaw Reservoir. The sky was a patchwork of heavy cloud. Droplets speckled the glass round the squash court.

They sat on leather chairs, each with a glass bottle of sparkling mineral water, sourced from the Swiss Alps. They hadn't showered, each dripping with sweat, still wearing white shorts, white collared T-shirts.

"All the times I've been here," said Canning, "it never stops bloody raining. You should do something."

Stapleton raised a quizzical eyebrow. "About the weather?"

"Yes. Have a chat with God. Tell him you're not impressed."

"Certainly. Though I doubt He'll listen. I rather like the rain. It reminds me."

"Of what."

"That the sun can't shine all the time."

Canning gave a tinny laugh. "Very philosophical, I'm sure. The answer to that is easy. Move to your new villa in Tenerife. You'll soon forget about the rain. Sun-filled hours every day, enjoying cocktails by the pool."

"Perhaps." Stapleton sipped from the bottle. Sparkling water, to his mind, was so much more invigorating than still. "How are we feeling?"

"We? As in me? Defeated. I'll have to improve my service game."

"It's your weakest link. And everything else?"

"Ah. You mean about later. I feel as I always feel at such times. Chilled. Relaxed. I have no issues. I know you bring me here to sound me out. And I understand completely. But you don't have to worry. I've never felt better." Canning raised his hands out, in mock drama. "See. Not a tremble. Steady as hard rock. Do I pass the test, Doctor?"

"This is good to hear," Stapleton said. He knew his friend had a habit. It was important he stayed clean before the operations, for obvious reasons. "We're getting four delivered. You take two, I'll take two. All going well, they should be neatly boxed and wrapped before breakfast tomorrow."

Canning's delicate face quivered into a smile, revealing sparkling white teeth. "You make it sound like Christmas."

Stapleton returned the smile. His teeth weren't just as perfect. Then again, he hadn't had implants. "But it is. And we're two Santas. Distributing our little gifts."

"Gifts? Really?"

"The gift of life. To those who need it."

"At a price."

"Indeed."

Canning pressed the cold bottle against the side of his face. "We give life, and we take life. I suppose there's a symmetry to that."

"A forty-million-pound symmetry. We can meet at the theatre at 2am? I don't expect them any earlier."

"Fine."

"Don't be late."

"Please."

Stapleton took another sip. "What will you do with your share?"

"New car, obviously. And property. You can never go wrong with property."

"May I suggest something else?"

"What?"

"Squash lessons."

They laughed, and a silence fell, each wrapped in their own thoughts.

35

Black gulped back the remains of his coffee, went to his room, packed what little he had in his sports bag, including the Desert Eagle and the assortment of other pistols he had collected over the last day. He was like a magnet. He attracted weapons, and all things bad.

He left, half expecting a clutch of suited gangsters to grab him, bundle him in a car. But there was nothing. Life went on. It was 7.45, and people were getting to work, going to the corner shop for milk, buying a newspaper. Doing things people do. He made his way to his car, where he'd left it the evening before, in a public car park. It was much fuller now. He got in, drove off.

Black drove the forty-five miles to Thorntonhall without the radio, absorbed in his own thoughts. He hardly knew Deborah's sons. He'd chatted, briefly, to the older one at the funeral reception. Chris. A young soldier in the parachute regiment. The younger one – Tony – had met him at the house with a solemn politeness, barely speaking. Twelve years old, if he recalled. A deep, intense boy. No wonder, his father shot to death in a country road.

Black got to Thorntonhall in just over an hour, competing

with the morning rush. He parked in the driveway. The lawn needed trimming. The flowers in the hanging baskets were dying of thirst. Weeds peeped up through the spaces in the coloured flagstones. The unmistakable taint of neglect.

Black got to the front door, which opened before he had the chance to ring the bell. Before him, Deborah Gallagher. How even just a few short days could change someone, he thought, when those days were filled with worry and fear. Her face was pale as death. Hollow-eyed. Cheekbones harsh and sharp. Her hair lank. She wore a pair of old jeans and a too-large woollen pullover, rendering her thin and fragile.

She had been crying.

"Come in, Adam. Thanks for coming."

He followed her into the kitchen.

"Coffee?"

"Sure."

He waited, silent. He watched her click the kettle, get a mug from a wooden mug-tree.

"What do you take?" Her voice was flat, listless.

"Just as it is."

She got a jar of Nescafé from another cupboard, opened it. She got a spoon from a drawer, put a spoonful of coffee in the mug. She stopped. The spoon dropped onto the marble unit. Her shoulders shook. She began to cry soft tears.

"Tell me what happened," Black said gently.

She took a deep breath, bit her lip, stemmed back more tears. "Let me get the fucking coffee. Please."

Black sat at the breakfast bar, on a high stool. The kettle boiled. She poured in the water, and placed it on the bar before Black. She sat opposite him.

"Thanks for coming. It means a lot."

Black smiled, sipped the coffee, waited.

"Things haven't been good lately." She gave a brittle laugh.

"As if you couldn't guess. I've been struggling. Everything's a struggle. Getting out of bed. Putting one foot in front of another. Taking a shower. Making a fucking cup of coffee. I guess you could say I've been a little self-consumed. Others might have called me a selfish bitch."

Black chose his words carefully. "Your husband died. You're grieving. You're only human, Debbie."

"I'm human all right." She fairly spat out the words. "And then some. One of my neighbours is a doctor. He got me some strong sedatives. I mean really fucking strong." She pointed to a cupboard next to a ranch-style double stove. "That's where I kept them." She looked at Black with tired frightened eyes. "How could I have known?"

Another sip of coffee.

"I've been half pissed most of the time, so it wasn't difficult. That's not true. Not half pissed. *Completely fucking pissed.* I guess when your mother is passed out on the sofa with a crate of wine in her stomach, looking like shit, then it's easy to see why you'd feel abandoned. Because that's exactly what I did. More or less. Abandoned my child. Abandoned Tony."

She was trying to tell him, but she couldn't focus. Black got that. Shock. Desperation. Guilt. A whole cocktail of raw emotion, making her thoughts wild, rambling.

"Tell me what happened."

She nodded, blinked away tears, took another deep breath, trying to compose herself.

Christ, this is killing her, thought Black.

"Yesterday, I went up to my son's room. He was in bed. He was lying in a pool of puke. He was unconscious. His lips were blue. His eyes..." A tremor passed through her face; she bit back more tears. "He'd found them. You understand? He'd found them."

Black understood, but he let her finish. She needed this, he knew. To get it out, like pus from a wound.

"He'd found the pills. So while Mummy was lying drunk, feeling sorry for herself, like a stupid selfish fucking bitch, he got the remnants of some gin I'd left lying about, and downed a whole fucking boxful of pills. And guess what."

Black waited.

"There's a hundred in a box."

A silence fell. Eventually Black spoke. His heart was heavy with dread. "How is he?"

"I've been in the hospital all night, at my son's side, where I should have been the minute after my husband was murdered. He came out of the coma this morning. He's unconscious, but he'll live. My son will live."

Black took her hand. There was hope after all. He thought of the fearless robin redbreast. "Then you can move forward. Take something from this. Something positive. Your son needs you. You need him. Sometimes, in the depths, when there's nothing but darkness, important things are easy to forget. But this has made you remember."

She gave a small tight smile. He smiled back. He meant what he said. She had two sons. Black once had a wife and daughter. Both dead. If he could have them back, he would never leave their side.

"I need to get back to the hospital soon," she said. She hesitated. The lines on her brow deepened, as if she had come to some inward decision. "He left a note." She got up, went to a drawer, opened it, took out an opened envelope, returned to her high stool, sat. She placed it delicately on the breakfast bar. "I'd like you to read it. Please."

Black looked at the envelope, at Deborah. "I'm not sure. This is personal. I have no place..."

"Please. I need someone just to make sense of everything. A shoulder to lean on. Your shoulder, Adam."

Black could offer no response. He picked up the envelope. It felt heavy in his hands. A young boy's last words to the world. He had no right to read such sacred text. But Deborah wanted him to share her burden. And Black was especially good at that.

He opened it. The paper was lined and cheap and torn from a notepad. There was nothing glamorous about a young boy's suicide note. He wrote this, and didn't give a damn about the quality of the paper. Three simple words, written neatly, in black biro.

All my fault.

Black carefully placed the note back in the envelope, put the envelope back on the breakfast bar.

"What does it mean?" Deborah searched Black's face, as if he were an oracle of sorts.

"I really don't know. But at least you can ask him."

"Does he blame himself, for his father's death? Or for something else. Why would he say that?"

Black said nothing.

"I'm scared, Adam. Things are happening too fast. My husband's dead. My son's in hospital. Chris is coming up later today. The Regiment's given him leave. Because of... well, everything. What if they come to the house?"

"They?"

"The people who killed my husband. Did you find anything about Remus? Did they kill Desmond? What about Charley Sinclair? Did he know anything?"

Her mood had changed. She was firing questions at him almost aggressively. Again, another symptom of profound shock. Black had witnessed its manifestations many times, in the battlefield, and after. PTSD. Post-traumatic stress disorder. In simple terms, an overwhelming mind-fuck.

He answered honestly, and gently. "I don't know who killed Desmond. Charley couldn't help. That was a dead end. I'm sorry, Deborah."

Her response was sharp. "So we don't know anything about this Remus Syndicate?"

Not yet, thought Black. He didn't respond.

Deborah's eyes welled up; a single tear trickled down her cheek. "I'm sorry, Adam. I'm finding this somewhat... difficult."

"There's nothing to be sorry about."

"Can you stay?" she asked suddenly. "For a few nights. So we can feel safe, just for a little while. You would be like an anchor in a shitstorm. I don't even know if that makes sense. I have a spare room."

Black nodded – what the hell else was he doing? If she felt safe with him about, then what harm was there. *Plenty.* He had a bag of guns in the boot of his car. Only hours earlier, he'd brought about the death of the head of a crime organisation. A young girl in Aberdeen had died in his arms. He was a source of trouble and mayhem. *Plenty could go wrong.* But Deborah Gallagher needed help, and Adam Black, being Adam Black, found such a plea impossible to refuse.

He smiled, sipped his coffee. "I'll take the couch."

36

Deborah had to get back to the hospital. She gave Black a spare key for the front door. Black also had matters to attend to. He said he would return to the house in the early evening. He drove straight to his office, where only the day before he'd killed two men, now both lying in the dirt in a forest in the middle of nowhere. But he had a little cleaning to attend to. The man called Mr Neville had pumped out a gallon of his blood on Black's office floor, as indeed had Daniel, when Black put a bullet in the side of his head.

Black reached his office. It was his secretary's day off, thankfully. He would struggle to explain why the carpet was awash with congealed blood.

Black, ever vigilant, waited in his car for twenty minutes before entering. There was no indication of menace. No parked cars with men inside. No loitering individuals on the street. Of course, if the surveillance team were good at their job, Black would never know. But he had a hunch. He understood violent men, and their habits. He guessed his name was now of no consequence to the gang once run by Malcolm Copeland.

Black entered the building, unlocked his office door. He got a mop and bucket, soaked up the blood, flushed it away. He wiped off the blood spatters on the wall, and segments of Daniel's skull, and bits of hair and brain. A gruesome task, but all things gruesome were old acquaintances of Adam Black. His clean up would never fool police forensics, but on casual inspection, it would do. He sprayed the room with some air freshener. The smell of death, once in the nostrils, never seemed to leave.

Black sat at his desk. He was weary. Long night. He pondered. The death of Desmond Gallagher seemed now to point in the direction of the Remus Syndicate, whatever the hell that was. They were the logical connection. Deborah had shown him a file with two threatening letters, the file marked under "Remus". It might be something. It might be nothing. No point in revisiting Charley Sinclair to ask him if he knew. Sinclair was dead, so Daniel had said. Black had no reason to disbelieve him.

Black didn't use a computer, but his secretary did. He went to her desk, in the reception room. He checked Companies House, searching "Remus". Over three hundred listings came up, ranging from kitchen installations to furniture restorers. He tried the Land Register, on the off-chance any property was in the ownership of Remus. It was a long shot. Nothing came up.

It was back to scratch. Black cursed his incompetence. He had been too quick to reach a conclusion. Sinclair had told Malcolm Copeland that his partner – Desmond Gallagher – knew about the money laundering, and was going to the police. Ergo, Copeland orders the execution of Gallagher. An easy conclusion to reach. Too easy. And all wrong.

Black rubbed his eyes, massaged his forehead, and thought, for the millionth time, of Penny Sinclair, dying in his arms, blood-soaked, the light fading from her eyes, and for the millionth time, wondered what the fuck God was doing, to entertain such a thing. But Black had given up on God a long time ago. The Desert Eagle was significantly more reassuring, and much more of a friend.

Black knew himself. He wouldn't stop. Not now. He would find out who killed Desmond Gallagher. He would find out about the Remus Syndicate. He would make it end.

Only two miles away, Haytham Bustan was finalising plans. The evening would be eventful, and busy. The Syrian family were currently in Nottingham, being taken in two separate cars on a leisurely journey north. There would be two stops, for food, and also for car changes. Bustan didn't expect them to arrive in his little Govanhill flat any earlier than 3am.

There, with the assistance of his interpreter, he would greet them, introduce himself in a gracious manner, explain how wonderful life was going to be, send the kids off for their pre-arranged appointments with the hospital, then kill the parents. Not that he would do the killing himself. His fat friend – Yousef Kaya – would see to that. With the help of a couple of other men, possibly. Kaya was an expert in efficient killing. Breaking a neck, slitting a throat. He lacked conscience. Bustan didn't care, particularly, about the manner of their deaths. What he did care about was the loss of income. He would otherwise have collected eighty grand for the parents. But those in charge – the Remus Syndicate – now wanted only children. Untainted goods. Bustan saw the logic. But the financial hit still irked him.

At the same time, four of his men would break into the house of Deborah Gallagher, stage a burglary, bludgeon her to death. He allowed himself a small, somewhat smug, smile. Equilibrium was maintained. The loss he sustained for the non-payment of the Syrian parents was balanced by the money he would collect for killing the woman. Not so bad, after all.

The men he had chosen were a different team from those who had broken into Charley Sinclair's house the previous evening. Each brought over from the slums of Istanbul. Two were distant relatives, as ever. Two were friends of friends. Each would kill a stranger for a nickel, and not look back.

Bustan and the four men were sitting hunched round a table in his little coffee shop on Victoria Road. They listened, while he instructed, their expressions deadpan. *Like talking to lizards*, thought Bustan. Same leathery skin, same lifeless eyes. All bone and sinew. Each possessing not one shred of empathy. The type of men Bustan could rely on.

As ever, the air was rich with tobacco smoke. They each drank tiny white cups of strong Turkish coffee, chain-smoking, listening.

Bustan directed his dialogue to one in particular. He called himself simply "Ringo". The story went, he'd killed a man with two Japanese Tetsubo war clubs, pounding the head and face like a drum, rendering it into a flat mush. The name "Ringo" stuck. He wore it, like a badge of honour.

Bustan gave him the address, complete with postcode, written on a piece of scrap paper.

"You make it messy," said Bustan. "Frenzied. Like you panicked, and lost control. You understand?"

Ringo regarded him, sloe-eyed, impassive. "Of course, Bustan. Frenzied. There will be no problem."

"And ransack the place. Jewellery. Any cash. Yes?"

Ringo's face broke into a cold grin. Bustan thought of a smiling skull. "Relax, Bustan. It will be taken care of."

"And if there should be anyone in the house..."

"Then we'll take care of it. Collaterals. Just bad luck."

"For them," said Bustan.

"Yes. For them."

37

Black used the front door key Deborah had given him. There was no alarm to worry about. From the office, he had gone back to his flat to collect clothes, overnight stuff. He remained cautious. But he entered and exited without trouble. He got to Deborah's house about 5.30. There was a note on the kitchen unit.

Thanks Adam. I'm at the hospital. There's food in the fridge. Help yourself. Thanks again x.

Black suddenly realised he was famished. He'd brought his holdall, which, amongst other items, still held the small arsenal of pistols he'd collected. The kitchen and living room was an open-plan design, spacious. He made his way through to the living room, where, only days earlier, he'd sipped red wine with other mourners. He dumped the holdall by a large corner sofa, testing its firmness with the palms of his hands. It would do. He'd slept in far worse places.

He went back to the kitchen, opened the fridge. She wasn't kidding. The fridge was stocked full, all the colours. Yellow, red, green. She liked the healthy stuff. Black, on the other hand, cared little about what he ate, as long as there was a modicum of taste, and there was enough of it.

A noise behind him. He turned. Chris stood at the kitchen door.

"Captain Black?"

"Chris. Good to see you. And it's Adam. Please."

Chris Gallagher went over, gave Black a strong handshake. He was five foot eleven, at a push. Dressed in civilian clothes. He was lean as a whippet, dark hair cropped, fresh-faced. His skin was imbued with an outdoor glow, so often the case with soldiers. His expression candid and clear. Instantly likeable. Black imagined, in the battlefield, such a young man would never leave your side.

"You're up to see your brother?" Black asked.

Chris nodded. "I got leave last night, and came straight up. I went to see him this afternoon."

"How is he?"

"He's talking. He can't remember much. The doctor said that might happen. Short-term memory loss. But he's well. He keeps falling asleep. Which is good, I think. Tony needs rest. And his own space. To clear his head. And time. You understand? To make sense of things, what with Dad gone."

"Of course."

"Mum's with him now. She'll be back soon. She said you were coming. Can I get you anything?"

"Why don't you put the coffee pot on. I'll fix us something to eat. You hungry?"

"Could eat a pickled rat."

"Pickled rat? Perhaps I can do better, though don't bet the house on it. My cooking skills are gloriously average."

"Then let me," said Chris. "You get the coffee, Adam. I'll cook some pasta."

Adam did exactly that, fixed coffee, sat at the breakfast bar, watched while Chris made himself busy, sticking a pot of fresh tortiglioni on the hob, chopping onions, slicing red peppers, cutting strips of bacon, a sprinkle of seasoning, some crushed garlic. He put a pot of water and a pan with some olive oil on the hob, turned it up high.

He seemed absorbed. Black understood. The boy needed the distraction. Anything would do. To keep his thoughts from dwelling on the spectre brooding in the back of his mind – his younger brother had tried to kill himself. It was there, an undisputable fact, like a block of wood, or a lump of stone. It would never go away. But if the mind was busy, or the hands, or the legs, then the block of wood could be ignored, for a little while.

Keep moving. Words ingrained into the mind, into the soul, by the harsh disciplinarians of the Special Air Service. And it worked. Stop to think, and it was easy for your world to implode. Mental health was as important to the fighting soldier as a fully loaded Heckler & Koch MP5. Black thought again of the village in Afghanistan, a fleeting image of a dead child, and he and his men did exactly as they had been taught. They kept moving. Forward. Always forward.

Black admired the young man's quiet composure. "Where did you learn to cook?" he ventured.

Chris laughed. "Who says I can cook?"

"Whatever you're doing, it looks impressive."

He turned his head, looked at Black, the laughter gone. "Looks can be deceiving."

Black said nothing. He sipped his coffee. No milk. No sugar. Strong. Chris had declined the offer, getting some juice from the fridge.

"You're stationed at Colchester Barracks?" Black said.

"For my sins. 2nd Battalion."

"1 Para. Special Forces Support Group. That's where I went after Sandhurst. The Airborne Brotherhood. There's nothing in the world quite like it."

Chris gave a small half-smile and, using a knife, swept the onions and bacon from the wooden chopping board into the hot pan of olive oil, causing an instant, appealing sizzle. He emptied the pasta in a pot of boiling water.

"They still talk about you, Adam. You're right up there. You, Paddy Mayne, John McAleese, Charles Bruce. The things you did. That's my dream. To be accepted by the Special Air Service."

Black refrained from telling him that being half psychotic was an essential prerequisite for the fighting man of the SAS. All he said was, "If you want it bad enough, you'll get there."

"I want it, for sure," Chris said, quietly, more to himself.

Black got a couple of plates, cutlery. The conversation lulled, as Chris fussed over the cooking. Ten minutes later, he dished the pasta into the plates.

"Got to get the pasta al dente," said Chris.

"Of course you do. Smells good."

"Reserve judgement. Until it hits the taste buds."

Black beckoned to the living room. "Let's sit."

They went through, sat with the plates on their laps.

Black wolfed the food down. He was starving. "Not half bad."

Chris picked at his food, put the plate to one side. "I'm glad you like it."

"I'm glad you made it. My culinary expertise extends to beans and toast, on a good day."

"Were you in Afghanistan, Adam?" Chris asked suddenly. The switch in the conversation took Black a little by surprise.

"The War on Terror. The Forever War, as we called it. I was. Helmand Province. And other places."

"I did a tour six months ago." Chris hesitated. "It's a fucking madhouse."

"If you let it. The trick is to switch off. If you can."

"How did you do it?"

"Do what?"

"Kill."

Black said nothing.

"To squeeze the trigger. End a life. Take everything from a man. Everything he had. Everything he's going to have."

"It's what we're trained to do," said Black gently. "To act. With violence, when necessary. Otherwise..."

"My dad was shot. Everything he had was taken from him. Shot four times and left on the road. My little brother lies in a hospital bed with his stomach pumped out. Everywhere I look, I see death."

Black had nothing to say.

"It's all my fault."

An echo of the words written by a twelve-year-old on a piece of scrap paper, after he'd swallowed a box of pills.

"Don't think like that," Black said. Chris was sinking into a maudlin state of mind. *No wonder.* Black tried to veer him onto a different path. "Your dad was murdered. He'd received threatening letters from something called 'Remus'. Remember what your dad did. He was a Human rights lawyer. A heavyweight. My suspicion is that somehow he fell foul of this organisation. Perhaps he was protecting a client. Perhaps he'd uncovered something which might have exposed or compromised Remus."

"Remus?"

"I've checked Companies House. There's a hundred companies bearing that name. I suspect this particular organisation won't be listed. A little too obvious. I've checked the Land Register. Blank. The next port of call would have been accessing your dad's files. But the police have taken everything he was working on. Right now his files and computers are stored away in sealed boxes in a locked evidence room in the basement of Police Scotland."

Already the young man's mood had shifted. *Keep moving.*

"My dad had a partner. Charley Sinclair. He came round to the house sometimes. He might know something?"

He might, thought Black, if he weren't dead. Compliments of Malcolm Copeland.

"I spoke to him. He didn't know anything."

"Maybe the police can help?"

"Maybe. But it might be that your dad, by the nature of his work, incurred the displeasure of powerful people. Which is exactly why your mother didn't go to the police. She's scared. And I think she has every right to be. Which is also why she's asked me to be here. She's worried that whoever killed your dad might feel the need to clean things up. In case your dad disclosed things. A husband and wife share secrets. Remus might still feel vulnerable."

Chris nodded slowly, blinking, as if his mind was computing the full impact of Black's theory.

"I don't mean to be blunt," Black continued. "And it might be completely wrong. But then it might be right. How long are you up for?"

Chris cleared his throat, gave Black a fixed stare. "It never crossed my mind that Mum might be in danger. I've got two weeks' leave."

"Then you'll be a welcome addition."

"What now?"

"You and your mum concentrate on getting Tony better. We watch. We wait."

The reality was, Black had no clear plan. But if Remus felt inclined to return, then Black was in exactly the right place. And he had a hunch they might. Why? Because it would make sense. Kill the husband. Kill the wife, just in case. Clean up and move on. As Malcolm Copeland did. A repeat performance.

It was what all the bad guys did. Kill, kill, kill.

And it was what Black did too.

38

The man nicknamed "Ringo" took orders from Bustan, but that didn't mean he liked it. They were distantly related. Along the lines of a second or third cousin. They came from the same district of Istanbul. Sarıgöl. Dirt poor, slum ridden, and the drug capital of Turkey. Most spent their lives trying to get out. Most didn't, unless prison or death could be counted. Ringo was lucky. He knew Bustan. And Bustan recognised Ringo's penchant for brutality. When Bustan needed something sticky done, Ringo was the man.

But that didn't mean he liked it. Ringo had his own designs. Bustan was useful. Bustan had given him a passage to the soft West. But Ringo was keen to flex his own muscles. Ringo wanted his own tribe. He would tolerate Bustan for now. And then, at some point in the future, he might give Bustan a little taste of the violence he ordered Ringo to do to others.

Such were the thoughts running through Ringo's mind as he parked a white van on the outskirts of Thorntonhall, on a grass verge beside thick foliage, at 3am. The van was stolen. Two hours from now, it would be abandoned and burnt out on a side road ten miles away, where four cars waited, to pick him and each of his men up. One man per car. Less conspicuous. One thing he gave Bustan credit for – he was a good planner. Ringo had learned a lot from him.

Thorntonhall was smaller than a village. More of a hamlet, set in the countryside, which made things a lot easier. No CCTV cameras. Big houses set apart from each other, where neighbours kept to themselves. The one thing about rich neighbourhoods, he had come to realise, was that they didn't give a flying fuck about each other, unless it was to outshine – a trophy car, a new extension, a bigger hot tub in the garden.

They crept along the narrow pavement. Four of them, keeping to the shadows. Four whispers in the night. The only illumination came from quaint Victorian-style lamp posts, all fancy wrought iron, set far apart. They looked nice, but were there for show only – ineffective when it came to lighting up the street.

Each man carried a black plastic bin bag, containing a crowbar, to be used to enter, and then used to kill. Ringo also carried a stiletto knife, tucked discreetly in a pocket adapted from the inner lining of his jacket. He knew the address. They got to the front driveway. They put on balaclavas, covering the face, except the eyes. The house was set back a little from the road. Low clouds blanketed the moon and stars, rendering all things to vague shapes and blots of deeper shadow. Perfect conditions. Easy job.

They made their way towards the house. Three cars were parked in the front driveway. Which might indicate more people in the house. Or it might not indicate anything at all. It hardly mattered. Collateral damage.

They went round the side, encountering a short wooden fence, about waist height, which they dealt with without difficulty. They got to the back garden. There, a conservatory, a large decking. They got to back patio doors. Sliding doors. They were always the easiest to force open. Not that much force was required. The slider was outside. Ringo inserted the sharp edge of the crowbar between the door frame and the door, at the bottom, diagonal to the latch, and pried upwards. By tilting, the latch on the door lowered, releasing it from the bracket. The noise was minimal – like a shoe scuffed on the ground. He wriggled the door open. They were in.

Deborah had arrived back about nine earlier that evening. Tony was recovering well, she had explained. Another day, two at the most the doctors reckoned, then he'd be allowed to go home. After that, a programme of counselling. But the prognosis, generally, was good. She'd brought back pizza, which she, Chris, and Black ate in the kitchen. Black had a single cold beer. Deborah had a single half glass of wine. Chris stuck to fresh orange juice.

To Black's mind, Deborah's mood had lightened. She clearly loved her son being there, which was understandable. Better there, than the mountains of Afghanistan. She chatted about anything and everything. All Black had to do was listen. She was still in mild shock, perhaps. Despite her exuberance, she still looked exhausted, her face wan and thin.

At 11pm, she excused herself and went to bed. Black and Chris watched some TV. A Netflix thing with swords and monsters. Black didn't own a television, hadn't for a long time. After watching what was on offer, he remembered why.

Chris went to bed at midnight, leaving Black on his own, with the couch and a blanket. Black had thought it wise to have the Desert Eagle close by his side, plus a Beretta. He switched the lights out, settled into the stillness of the night, and fell into a sort of half-sleep, instilled by countless nights behind enemy lines, a part of the mind constantly awake, one hand a twitch away from a loaded weapon.

Just after 3am. A noise from the other end of the kitchen. Black woke instantly, senses sharpened to a pinpoint level of ability. He eased himself from the couch, picked up the Eagle, its solid weight an instant comfort. He took a careful step back, into a corner, to a deeper shadow, and watched.

Four figures emerged, morphing from the dark, quiet as a brush of cloth, outlines only. Also, outlines of weapons in their hands. Tooled up and ready to inflict a little damage. More than a little. Black didn't move, didn't breathe. He felt no fear. If his heart rate were checked at that moment, it wouldn't be a beat past fifty-five. Black was able to compartmentalise his emotion. Package it, seal the package, bury it somewhere deep. In its place a hollow, professional, detachment. Which was why, when it came to killing, Black had no issues. Provided the right guy got killed.

They crept their way forward, slowly, slowly. Four sinister shapes. Tentative. They were adjusting their sight to the interior darkness of the house. They got to the middle, by the breakfast bar. Stopped. They had a choice. They could keep moving directly forward, to the living room, towards Black. Beyond that, the conservatory.

They could change direction, creep out the kitchen through a door to their left, and into the main hall, leading to the front of the house, and to the stairs to the upper level. They wouldn't know the layout, Black presumed. Better to keep in a straight line, get a feel for the place. Once they'd cased the ground floor, they'd head upstairs, for the serious business. Where the bedrooms were.

Which is what they did. They moved forward, in unison, into the living room. Closer. Black made ready. Suddenly, the kitchen was ablaze with light. Another figure at the door to the hall. Deborah. In her dressing gown. Maybe she'd heard something too. Maybe she'd come down to get a drink. Maybe anything. Black didn't have time to consider. She screamed. The four men sprang back, startled. To one side, Deborah. Before them, standing in a corner, Black, pointing the Desert Eagle. Ringo, who was closest to the door, was the quickest to react. He darted towards Deborah. Something glittered in his hand. He grabbed her, pulled her close, held her in front, one arm embraced round her chest, a knife held at her throat.

"Drop the fucking gun!"

Black stepped forward. The four men were small, sinewy, wearing dark track bottoms, dark close-fitting tops, balaclava hoods. Each bearing metal crowbars. Nothing random here, Black thought. They had come with a purpose. And the purpose was easy to guess.

"Drop the fucking gun!" The man spoke with an accent. Eastern. The other three remained motionless, eyes set on Black.

Black cocked his head, as if bewildered. "Why?"

"What? Why the fuck do you think! I'll slit her throat."

Black gave the slightest shrug. "Do it. I don't care. But the moment you draw blood, you're finished. No more cards to play. And then I fire this Desert Eagle into your head. Then I'll kill your friends."

"You're bluffing."

"Really? Here's the deal. You let her go. I'll let you and your pals walk out of here. Unharmed. I just need you to answer a couple of questions."

Read a man's eyes, thought Black. The eyes tell a lot. Fear, worry, surprise. Black read this man's eyes, and saw nothing. Which meant a lack of empathy. Which meant trouble.

"Here's what I think," said the man, his accent heavy, but his English good. "I think you're full of bullshit."

Black said nothing. He could hit the three others no problem. Three easy kill shots. The fourth – the one holding Deborah – was problematic. The Desert Eagle was powerful, but not quite a precision instrument. And with the silencer attached, its accuracy diminished further. A millimetre out, less even, and it was Deborah's brains decorating the living room walls. Also, he had a strong feeling he'd meet a swift end if he relinquished the pistol. A rock and a hard place. More like the devil and a shitstorm.

Black gave a cold smile. Something suddenly increased his odds.

He sidestepped to his left, then again. The men, instinctively, manoeuvred their bodies to their right, including the man holding Deborah, who shuffled round so his back was to the door to the hall.

"Put the fucking gun down!" barked the man.

"If I do it, you'll promise not to hurt me?"

The man said nothing.

"I need that promise. Preferably a pinkie promise."

"What?"

Black held the pistol out before him, turned his wrist so the barrel pointed at the ceiling, gesturing surrender. Slowly, he bent down, as if to place the pistol on the living room floor. He glanced at Deborah, her face white as death, eyes round and wide. She would feel the blade on her neck, feel the man's body touching hers, and wonder if this was the last moment of her life.

"That's good," the man said.

"I'm glad you think so." Black twitched his head, the slightest nod. There was sudden movement at the door. A figure darted in, arm raised. A dull wet thud as Chris Gallagher brought a hammer down hard on the back of the man's head. He crumpled like a dry sack. Deborah, released from his grasp, leapt away. Black stood, calmly re-aimed the pistol at the three men. They wavered, rocking on their feet. Should they try an attack? Should they run? Should they stay put? Black read their indecision, and wondered if they were mad enough to try something. Or stupid. Or desperate.

"Please," Black said. "Try it. I'm in a killing mood."

They remained still.

"That's very wise."

Deborah had backed against a wall of the living room, standing semi-slumped, breathing heavily, one hand round her neck, where the blade had touched her skin. "What the hell's happening?" Her voice was low and hoarse.

Her son stood above the fallen man, hammer in his right hand, poised and ready for any sudden surge of movement. But the guy was on the ground, legs and arms sprawled, oblivious to the world. Blood was seeping out the back of his balaclava, forming a small pool on the floor. Either he was unconscious, or dead. Black hoped for the former. He had questions to ask, and answers to get.

"Just shows you how versatile a hammer can be."

Chris gave a frosty smile. "I heard the commotion. There's a toolbox in the garage. I thought it might be useful."

Black, weapon still trained on the three men, addressed Deborah. "I think these men were sent to finish a job. Let's ask them." He gazed at them, rotated the gun so that his aim rested on each one for three seconds. "Take your masks off." No movement. One of them raised his hands, started speaking in short urgent staccato bursts, in a language Black didn't instantly know.

Black shook his head. "I don't understand."

The man continued, his voice rising to a pleading whine.

"I don't believe our friends have a grasp of the English language." He flicked a glance at Chris. "Let's see their handsome faces."

Chris went over, pulled off each balaclava. Three faces stared back at Black, or more specifically the barrel of the Desert Eagle. Swarthy complexions, dark hair, hard leathery skin, eyes like flints. Each possessed the same look. A look Black had seen many times. Fear. Pointless asking such men anything. Low-ranking gang members with little to offer. The one on the floor however...

"Do you have any rope in the garage, Chris?"

Deborah answered. "There's shelves of stuff. Not sure about the rope. But I think there's heavy-duty sealing tape. Will that do?"

"Even better."

"I'll get it," Deborah said.

The man on the floor was stirring. A low moan emanated from beneath his hood. Chris strode over, pulled it off. The hair on the back of his head was slick with blood. The man struggled to his hands and knees, wobbled, collapsed back to the floor. He groaned. Black was mildly surprised he was still alive, and hoped, if he were to die, it wouldn't be too soon. Black had questions to ask.

Deborah returned with two full rolls of heavy-duty duct tape. Chris brought through four dining chairs from another room and arranged them in a line. At the point of Black's Desert Eagle, the three men standing were gestured to sit, which they did without complaint, and Chris bound their wrists to the armrests, and their ankles to the chair legs, winding the tape tight, rendering them immobile.

He lifted the fourth man up and dumped him onto the

remaining chair, repeated the process. The man stared ahead, glassy-eyed, slack-faced. He was still in a daze. Concussion. Possibly a fractured skull. Deborah, a little back, said nothing, watchful.

Black appraised the fourth man.

"Your English is good," he said. The man lifted his head a fraction, managed an inarticulate mumble. Black moved closer, snapped his fingers two inches from the man's eyes.

The man gave a weak smile, revealing a crooked row of nicotine-stained teeth, and said, "Fuck you."

"Not nice." Black casually slapped him across the face. Deborah, standing behind him, took a sharp intake of breath. *Needs must*, thought Black. If she didn't like it, she could leave the room. But she remained quiet. The man shook his head, absorbed the blow.

"What's your name?" asked Black.

"What are you going to do to us," replied the man. His eyes tilted up, focused, regarding Black.

"I could do any number of things. I could execute each of you. Stick the gun to your heads, squeeze, and then eternal darkness. Or perhaps you're a believer, and expect to get fast-tracked to paradise. Either way, you end up dead. But that's a road you don't need to go down. Things can be much easier."

The man said nothing.

"Let's start again – what's your name? And be polite. There's a lady present."

"I don't feel well. I need a doctor."

"That's for later. Let's dwell on the present for now. What's your name?" Black leaned closer. He lowered his voice. "I won't ask a third time."

The man licked his lips, eyes darting from Black to the massive handgun Black was holding. Debating. The man made the right choice.

"Ringo. They call me Ringo."

"Cute. Where are you from?"

"Turkish."

"You're Turkish? Nice. Hope you like our country. And I guess, Ringo, these three handsome fellows are your men. You're the commander, yes?"

The man cast a look to his left, to the others. "Yes."

Black nodded, smiled. "Now we're getting places." He had a hunch. It might come to nothing, but instinct told him Ringo was clever and cunning. And ambitious. "My guess, Ringo, is that like your men, you follow orders from someone above you. You were told to come here."

Ringo twitched his shoulders into something approaching a shrug. "Could be."

"And I get that. And I get that you're loyal to whoever that person is. Because without loyalty, what have we got? Chaos. You understand that word?"

"I understand."

"But the thing is, the guy who told you to do this is probably right now all tucked up in bed, nice and warm. Do you think he cares what happens to you? I'll bet, should things go badly for you tonight, he'll find a replacement in ten seconds flat. That's because, Ringo, you're *expendable*. You understand that word?"

Ringo stared at Black. He understood.

"But you know what I like to ask. What if. Two little words. But full of potential. What if, the guy who gave you the command to come here, didn't give commands anymore?"

The skin on Ringo's forehead furrowed in puzzlement. But Black saw something else. A glimmer of possibilities in his eyes. "What do you mean?"

"What if your boss – the guy who put you here, on this chair, staring at the barrel of a Desert Eagle – disappeared. No longer existed. Vanished. I wonder, if such a thing were to happen, who would fill his place?"

The man blinked. Black saw it clear as broad daylight. Scenarios running through Ringo's head. All good. All to his advantage.

"Here's the way I see it," continued Black. "You give me this guy's name, and where I can find him. Let me do the hard work."

The man reacted in the way Black had hoped for – a miniscule nod of the head.

"And then?"

"And then you let me take care of things."

"What about me? About us?"

"There has to be a bit of down payment. If something's too easy, then it's not worth having. You broke in. It's called 'burglary'. We phone the police. Sure, you might do a small stretch, but get the right lawyer and it could be months before you see a trial. All you have to do is nothing, except tell me his name, and where I can find him. And why you were sent here. Because I know, tooled up as you are, you didn't come to steal a little jewellery."

"You're making my head hurt," said Ringo. "What will you do to him?"

"Your boss?"

"Yes."

"Bad things."

"Why? What's it to you?"

"Let's call me an interested party."

"How do I know this isn't all bullshit?"

Black raised himself up, a formidable figure. Six two, muscular build, a cannon of a gun held in a hand like a shovel.

"Do I look like I'm talking bullshit." He waited, letting the words and image absorb. Then said, "I'm giving you a deal. A good deal. If you choose not to take it, then listen to my words,

Ringo. I'll put several bullets in your face, cut your body into bits, pack them in the boot of my car, and bury them somewhere deep. This is the reality you're in. So what do you say?"

Ringo blinked and twitched. Sweat dribbled into his eyes. Eventually, he spoke. "Bustan. His name's Bustan. He's at his flat in Govanhill. He's meeting people there tonight."

"Address?"

"Eighteen Westmoreland Street. Top right."

"Why did he send you here?"

"To kill the woman. Make it look like a robbery."

Black heard Deborah gasp.

"Why?"

"I don't know. Ask Bustan."

"Thank you," Black said. "If I find you're lying, then I'll kill you. Understand?"

"Yes."

Black turned to Deborah and her son, handed Chris the Desert Eagle. "Call the police. Report an attempted burglary. They broke in, you took them by surprise, subdued them, tied them up. If I were you, when the police get here, I'd lose the weapon."

"One man subdues four guys with crowbars?"

Black gave a wintry grin. "You're in the parachute regiment. Which makes you superhuman."

"These people were sent to kill me," said Deborah, her voice hollow, her cheekbones harsh in the glare of the kitchen lights. "If you hadn't been here, what then? What if Tony was here?"

"They were sent to kill you *all*," replied Black bluntly. "Not just you. These men are foot soldiers. I need to go up a level. I need to meet the man who gives the orders."

"Will you make this end, Adam?"

"Yes."

"What now?"

"Time to hunt."

Black left the four men in the care of Chris Gallagher, who was more than capable, ensuring Chris called the police. Black took with him the two Berettas from his sports bag.

He had an address. He had a name.

Bustan.

39

Events were running as planned, and Haytham Bustan was pleased. The Syrian family had just arrived, and had been escorted to the front living room by the translator, Mehmet Aksoy. Bustan could hear their conversation through the thin walls. Aksoy's fluent voice, soothing, warm. The responses from the parents. Tired, but happy. Bustan didn't understand the language, but he understood the mood behind it. They were refugees, saved from hell, and now in paradise, the free West, where women were allowed an education, where people were rewarded if they worked hard, where racism was a crime. Paradise.

Not quite, thought Bustan. It was 3.30am. He'd phoned the mobile number given to him by the Remus Syndicate, as he always did. Different number every time. *They're here.* The voice – always heavily disguised, transformed into something outlandish by a voice modulator – acknowledged his message. A vehicle would be there to pick them up in an hour. *Remember*, said the voice. *Only the children.*

In the kitchen with Bustan was Yousef Kaya, enlisted for his skills in such matters. There were two others, both strong and dependable. Bustan would arrange for the children to leave first. Once gone, he would deal with Mum and Dad. Guns were messy. Strangulation, though slower, was neater all round. No blood on the carpet or the furniture. Then, once dead, matters were finalised in a controlled fashion. Tarpaulin sheets spread on the bathroom floor, the bodies placed in the bath, and then the limbs removed, any mess washed away. The parts transferred into industrial strength bin bags, and then removed to a place far away. Bustan, by that time, would be long gone.

They were sitting around a cheap wooden table. The kitchen door opened. Aksoy popped his head in.

"Okay, Bustan."

Bustan stood, regarded the three men at the table. "Be ready."

He went through to the living room. Two adults, four children. Two boys, two girls. According to the records, the girls were twins, ten years old, and the boys five and six. Both the boys were sleeping, wrapped together in a duvet cover, oblivious to the world. The older kids were awake, but pale. Dressed in matching pink pullovers with a smiling face of Mickey Mouse across the front. Cheap blue jeans, cheap sandals. Thin blue raincoats.

The four kids were on one couch, the parents on another. The parents likewise were dressed in cheap clothes. Unbranded jogging bottoms, oversized pullovers, worn fleeces. At their sides, their possessions packed in two threadbare holdalls, and several white plastic bags. They'd been given food – a KFC bucket of chicken and bags of chips, and some juice, the remnants of which were scattered across a central coffee table.

Bustan sat on a chair opposite. Aksoy stood beside him. The family were Kurdish. Bustan commenced his opening spiel. *Welcome to Scotland...*

They listened, Aksoy translating, a beaming smile never

leaving the woman's face. Like all the faces Bustan met here, in this little room, in his little flat in Glasgow. Faces expressing hope and sheer undiluted gratitude.

Bustan continued, "But we must get you to hospital," he said. "For check-ups. To keep you healthy. Good for your children, yes?" *Yes! Yes! Yes!*

"We'll take your children first. You'll be following. Yes?"

The mother's face flickered briefly with doubt.

"You don't need to worry," Bustan reassured her, his voice deep, almost melodic. "Only for a short while. You'll meet them at the hospital. We'll take care of everything."

The father spoke. He'd travelled thousands of miles to get here, used all his money, had nothing to go back to, and had passed the point of no return. No way was he raising any complaints, nor would he allow his wife to. If the kids had to go separately, then that was fine. To stay meant survival. To go back meant death.

Bustan knew all the signs, had seen it played out many times before. They were vulnerable. It was their vulnerability which made them such easy targets. He nodded like a wise old sage.

"Good," said Bustan. "The hard bit's done. From now on, everything is sunshine." Bustan gave a rumbling laugh. "Or maybe not, with the Scottish weather."

Aksoy translated. Father laughed. Mother also laughed, but with a tinny undertone. She was still worried about being separated from her kids. *Tough shit*, thought Bustan.

Bustan's mobile pinged. Text message. *Car outside.*

Bustan stood. "Time to go," he said. "The great adventure begins."

The father picked up one of the little boys, the mother the other, the kids hardly reacting, both in a deep sleep. They went out, the older girls following, silent and solemn, Aksoy leading, like a procession from the Pied Piper. One of the girls suddenly darted towards Bustan, gave him a hug. "Thank you," she said. Bustan patted the back of her head, like an affectionate uncle, thinking, *You're worth £40,000 cash, so the pleasure's all mine.*

They left the flat. Bustan watched from the bay window in the living room. The older girls took their younger brothers, and they got into the back of a dark SUV. The father shut the car door, the mother leaning close to the car window, smiling, waving, blowing kisses. *Touching*, thought Bustan. The car drove off. Aksoy led the parents back into the building.

Bustan sat and waited. He took the opportunity of opening a new packet of cigarettes. He scrunched the cellophane wrapper into a ball and tossed it into the chicken bucket left on the coffee table. He teased out a cigarette, pulled a plastic lighter from his pocket, and lit up. Capstan. Unfiltered. Turkish cigarettes were good, but Capstans had teeth, made the lungs feel every inhalation.

Thirty seconds later, the parents entered the room. Bustan beckoned them to sit, which they did. Aksoy stood to one side, face impassive. Bustan had primed him as to what was to occur. Aksoy had accepted it with indifference – he was well paid, so didn't give a damn. As long as he got his envelope of cash at the end of the night.

This was a new phase. Up until now, the whole family was bundled off, parents and kids, and Bustan's role was finished. But a new element had been introduced, and if it went well, then he would adopt the same procedure for each occasion a family was brought up.

He drew in a deep drag of tobacco, savouring the taste.

"Don't worry," he said. "Your beautiful children will be fine. Another car will be here in five minutes, to pick you up, then happy reunions."

Aksoy relayed the words in a flat, robotic tone. They smiled, nodded.

"It's been a very long trip," Bustan continued. "You must be tired. Soon, you'll have your own room, and then you can wash and sleep."

The father said, "I haven't slept for days. At least it feels like that. The boat trip was the worst. We were scared we'd get caught." Aksoy translated. Bustan again put on his wise owl nodding response. "All your troubles are behind you. No more worry. A new chapter awaits." *Which, in a sense, was true.*

Bustan got up. "I have to leave the room for a minute with my friend Aksoy. But we'll be back soon."

He and Aksoy left the room, closing the living room door behind them. They went into the kitchen, the next room just along the short corridor.

Bustan addressed the three men. "It's time. Make it clean. No mess."

They stood, Yousef Kaya's massive bulk dominating the room. The two smaller men beside him held knives and nylon cord. It was 4am and Bustan wanted to get to his bed. This part of the procedure, he would gladly leave to others.

Suddenly, a knock on the front door. More than a knock. Three knocks. But louder. Like someone had banged it with something hard. Intending to be heard. Bustan jerked round, remained motionless. They all did. This was not expected. This was new. He waited. He counted in his head. Ten seconds passed.

Then it happened again. Three loud knocks. Bustan almost jumped. He raised a finger to his lips, indicating absolute silence. Again, he counted. Fifteen seconds. Then three more raps on the front door. Whoever it was, wasn't going away. Which meant it had to be dealt with. He stubbed his cigarette on the kitchen tabletop, nodded to the two men bearing the knives and cord, and gestured with his head. *Answer it.*

They acknowledged the gesture, made their way through the

hall. Bustan watched from the kitchen. They got to the front door. It was solid wood, unglazed. Impossible to know who was on the other side. One of the men leaned forward, listening.

His accent was heavy and broken. "Who's there?"

Silence. He waited, his friend behind him. "Who's there?" he repeated. Nothing. He looked over his shoulder, to Bustan, who gave a sharp nod. *Open it.*

The lock was a standard mortice. Also, fastened at head height, a solid chain lock. The man took a key from his pocket, inserted it in the keyhole, turned it. He opened the door carefully, by the maximum distance the chain lock allowed. All of four inches. He peered out. He turned again to Bustan, who still stood at the kitchen doorway. The man raised his shoulders, perplexed, the motion meaning – *I can't see anyone, so what do I do?*

Bustan again gave a sharp nod. *Open it!*

The man understood. He closed the door gently, slid the chain off the track. He paused. In one hand he held his knife – a fixed blade hunting knife. Seven inches of steel, serrated edge. He raised it, poised. Bustan watched, breath held.

The man opened the door.

40

Come not between the dragon and his wrath.
— *King Lear:* William Shakespeare

Black knew the street. Knew *of* the street. Part of a wider area designated by Scottish Government to house refugees, and as such, a place often in the news, usually involving hate crime. It was only a couple of miles from his office, in the south of Glasgow, about nine miles from Deborah's house. It was after 3am, and the traffic was virtually zero. The occasional taxi.

Black had no idea what to expect. He had no real plan, other than a strategy of direct action, if such could be described as a plan. Engage with the enemy, see what happens. Hardly subtle. But subtlety had never been Black's strongpoint. The whole thing could end up a waste of time and effort. Ringo could be lying, a final *fuck you.* But Black thought not. Ringo was hungry. He wanted higher up the food chain, and saw Black as the means by which this could happen.

Black got to Westmoreland Street at 3.40am. Long Victorian tenements on either side, red sandstone, tall bay windows, high peaked slate roofs. Once, long ago, a good place to live. But over the years, slum landlords acquired flat after flat, increasing their portfolio, contributing nothing to maintenance and repair, the buildings descending into squalor. Now a shit place to live.

Vehicles were parked on both sides, making the road manageable for two cars, just. Black drove at a crawl, eyes searching for number eighteen. There! Painted white on the stone, two numbers. He looked up. Ringo had said top right. The curtains were closed, but light peeped through. Someone was in. Maybe Bustan, in the middle of his "meeting".

He picked his speed up, drove on a hundred yards, found a space, and parked. He took out one of the Berettas from his sports bag, tucked it in the belt of his jeans, covered it with his leather bomber jacket. He made his way back, the street lights casting a dreary orange glow. The world was silent at this time, frequented by such frightening people as Ringo, and Bustan. And Adam Black.

He arrived at the main communal entrance. The buzzer control system, like all the other main doors on the street, was broken, allowing anyone to enter and exit at will. He went in. A single sconce on the wall provided illumination. The floor was cold grey stone, as were the walls, decorated with splurges of meaningless graffiti.

Doors on either side. Two on each level, four levels, including the ground floor. No names on the doors. Black made his way up, treading softly, quiet as a cat. He got to the top floor. Two doors. The door he wanted was to his left, looking from the building to the street. It was solid wood. He pressed his ear to the grain, listening. All quiet.

He stepped back. He pulled out the Beretta. It was an M9, with a fifteen-round staggered box magazine. More than enough fire power. He hoped. Unlike the Desert Eagle, it lacked a silencer. He really didn't wish the neighbours lurching from their beds to the sound of gunshots. He hoped the sheer presence of a semi-automatic pistol would be enough.

He took a deep calming breath. He flipped the pistol, banged the door with the grip. Hard. Three times. He stepped to the side, stood, back flat against the wall, raised his arm straight in front, aimed.

He waited.

He counted to ten, repeated the process. Three hard raps.

He resumed his stance, waited.

Nothing. Black pictured the scene inside. Sudden silence. Frantic gestures. Worried faces. He counted to fifteen, repeated, resumed his position. He sensed movement, from the interior. The unmistakable creak of floorboards. Someone was approaching the door, as unobtrusively as possible.

Black waited.

A key turning. Black exhaled slowly, focused on the moment. The door opened. Not by much, restricted by a chain lock. Whoever was looking through the gap would see little, vision minimised to what was directly if front, narrowed to several inches wide.

A voice. Foreign. Turkish, guessed Black. Friends of Ringo.

"Who's there?"

Black remained still.

The door closed. Black heard the slide of the chain being released. The door opened. The first thing to emerge was a seven-inch blade. Attached to its handle, a hand. Attached to the hand, the sleeve of a blue shirt.

A man emerged. He sensed Black's presence. He half turned, gasped, staring straight into the muzzle of Black's Beretta. The man stood, rooted. The stab of a knife would never outrun the speed of a bullet, especially when the bullet was fired from a gun six inches from the face.

Black motioned the man into the flat. The man backed in, Black following. Black noted, in his other hand, a coil of nylon cord. Another man stood in the corridor, eyes wide in surprise, also clutching a knife and cord. At the end of the corridor, a kitchen. Standing in the doorway, a third man, and behind him two others, one obesely fat. Each face an image of startlement. Black almost found it amusing.

No one spoke. Black closed the front door, kept walking, which meant the man staring at the point of his gun had to back off, as did his colleague in the corridor.

Black stopped halfway. Doors to his left and right. Keeping the pistol trained on the first man, he tried the door to his left. It opened, revealing an empty room, devoid of any furnishings.

"Keep moving," said Black, his voice low. The first man nodded, both hands raised above his head.

"Sure, big guy," he said, his accent heavy, the surprise in his face turned to an air of casual insolence. "Anything you say."

They weren't scared. Men well used to violence.

He moved forward, the two men before him shuffling back, like some awkward dance routine. Black reached his hand out, to try the door on his right. The front living room, guessed Black, facing the street.

Suddenly the door opened. Before him, a woman. Wearing a thin rain jacket, cheap track trousers. She saw Black, gun in hand. She reacted as any normal human being would.

She screamed.

Chaos ensued. Black was distracted. The man saw an advantage. He swiped his arm down, trying to knock the gun to one side. Not quick enough. Black fired. The noise was sharp, echoing in the close confines of the flat, like a whip crack. The man's face disintegrated into a froth of blood and bone. The woman's scream reached a frenzied pitch.

The man slumped into Black. Black now had no clear shot. He pushed him to the side. Too late. The second man leapt forward, batted the pistol from Black's hand. It clattered to the floor. The man raised his arm, swung down, knife poised to penetrate Black's chest. Black put one foot back, bent the knees to maintain stability, brought his forearms up, crossing them, blocking the thrust. Textbook manoeuvre.

Black half swivelled, powering up from his legs, struck with his elbow, a vicious blow under the chin, breaking jaw and teeth. The man's head flicked back. Black followed up with a knee to the groin. The man folded forward. Black caught the back of the man's head, connected face with upraised knee. The man dropped, dazed, the entire sequence of events taking less than four seconds. Exactly as Black had been trained.

The fat man came clambering from the kitchen, his bulk as wide as the hall. Two hundred and seventy pounds easy. Loose jogging trousers, a pale-yellow vest. A bullet head, bald as a stone, incongruously small on massive round shoulders. A clear three inches than Black. Clamped in one meaty fist, a machete.

The taller man swung, surprisingly fast. Black ducked, aimed a blow to the stomach. Whether the man felt pain was impossible to say. The machete was useless at close quarters, but neither did Black wish to get too close, and risk being squeezed by those great arms. Black leapt back.

Once again, the machete flashed down. Black dodged to one side. His left hand darted out, a jab to the man's face. The man grunted, swung again, a shimmering arc. Black ducked a second time, the blade a whisper above his hair. Black reared up, struck, a sledgehammer blow to the man's right eye. The man jerked his head, as if dismissing a fly. Black retreated two steps, light on his feet. The man hacked again.

This time Black attempted to catch the wrist, and perform a lock, the purpose to snap the ulna. The force was too great, the angle wrong. The wrist slipped from his grasp. The man lashed down with his other hand, attempting to punch Black on the back of the neck. Black drove instantly forward, ramming his shoulder into the man's waist. The man pulled his knee up, battering Black's chest, the breath knocked from his lungs. Black caught the knee, shifted, caught the ankle, twisted.

The man howled, hopped to one side, at the same time sending a buffeting blow to the side of Black's head. Black reeled against the corridor wall, disoriented. The man tried to regain balance. Black sent another solid right-handed punch to the face, targeting the right eye, which was shut, the left eye swollen.

The man roared out, dropped the machete, lurched forward, his great arms surrounding Black. Black kicked at the man's knee, heard something click. The leg gave way, the man fell. Black fell with him, jabbing his elbow into the exposed neck. The man spluttered, fighting for breath, Black astride him, still clenched in his arms. Black butted chin, nose, all the time the man heaving and lurching, like some monstrous whale.

The man's grip loosened. Black leant over, grabbed the fallen machete, raised it high, plunged it through the chest, deep, to the hilt. The man spasmed, went limp.

Black staggered to his feet, panting and sweating. Two men remained in the kitchen, motionless, faces registering a combination of shock and fear, their exit having been blocked by the flailing bodies of Black and his opponent. The woman was still at the door to his right, joined by a man. Her screams had stilled. She stared at Black, stricken.

Black appraised the two men directly before him, raised himself up, machete in one hand, dead men at his feet, a wound to his head. A formidable figure.

"I'm looking for a man called Bustan."

41

Black calmly picked up the Beretta. Time was limited. The screams, the gunshot – he expected the police within ten minutes. Perhaps fifteen at a push. Hope for the best, prepare for the worst. Get set for a speedy exit.

Black knew fear, and everything about it. He saw fear in the faces of those around him. The initial three men he had encountered were different. Men acquainted with violence, and as such, almost inured to fear. Like Black. But the two in the kitchen were different. Softer. Scared. Men who gave the orders, rather than carried them out. And the man and woman? He had no real idea about them, other than they were terrified. A good place to start.

He aimed the pistol at the woman, her face clenched and tight. He moved the pistol a fraction, to the man at her side.

"Bustan?" The man frantically shook his head. The woman suddenly spoke, pointed a trembling arm to one of the men standing in the kitchen doorway.

"Bustan," she whispered. "Bustan."

"Thank you."

Black turned his attention to the two men. "Good evening,

gentlemen. Or should I say good morning. Hope I haven't barged in."

He walked towards them. They backed into the kitchen interior. Black kept his gaze on the man called Bustan. A squat man, receding dark hair oiled back like a wave, lined leathery face, heavy wrinkles around the eyes and lips. A tinge of pale orange discolouration to the face. A sure sign of a chain-smoker. He raised both hands in placation, spoke in perfect English. His voice was frantic.

"What is it you want? Money, yes? How much are they paying you? I can double it, for sure. Did they send you?"

Black responded with a cold smile. *Keep talking.* "They've paid me a lot of money, Bustan."

"Sure they have. I can treble it. Cash. What did I do wrong?"

Black took a gamble. "When the Remus Syndicate gives orders, it's wise not to ask."

Bustan's voice rose to a pitch. "Is it the kids? Were there not enough? I can get more. No problem. They're getting four tonight. I can get them four every night. No problem. Tell them. I can give them whatever they want."

Black lowered his pistol, spoke in a soft voice. "What?"

"And the parents," Bustan continued, words tumbling over each other. "We can get rid of them. We were going to do that, just as they wanted. I've never let the Syndicate down. They ask for something, Bustan delivers. Always. Why is this happening!"

Black's voice remained low, and perfectly calm. "You were going to get rid of them?"

"Yes! Those two!" This time it was Bustan's turn to point a trembling finger, to the man and woman standing in the doorway beside Black. "Yousef was gifted in such matters. All clean. No mess. Until you killed him. Please! Tell them. I can get lots more kids."

Black took a deep breath, trying to scale the enormity of

what Bustan was saying. He turned his gaze to the man beside Bustan, who hadn't spoken a word. He was tall, wire thin, rough shaven, a hook nose, sharp cheekbones.

"You," Black said. "What is your role in this?"

The man swallowed, swallowed again, and like Bustan, spoke in good English. "I interpret. I swear. It's all I do. What goes on here has nothing to do with me."

"Really. But yet you know it happens. What's your name?"

"Mehmet Aksoy."

Black turned his attention back to Bustan. Clock was ticking. He needed answers. "What goes on here. Clarify, if you will."

Bustan attempted bluster. "I can phone right now. Get this all sorted. A mistake's maybe been made, yes?"

"Answer the question."

"Let's talk about this, reasonably. Let me make the call."

"You need to focus, Bustan."

There were three men at Black's feet. One shot, one stabbed. Both dead. The third was only concussed, and was struggling to get to his feet. Black casually adjusted his aim, and shot him in the head. The woman put her hands to her face, gave a stifled scream.

Black brought his aim back to Bustan. "I hope I have your attention."

Bustan's lip quivered. Words gushed forth. "I bring people here. Refugees. Illegals. Usually from Syria, Afghanistan. Places like that. Bad places." He hesitated. "Then they leave."

"Where!"

"The Remus Syndicate handles things after they go."

"Where!"

"To the hospital."

Black's voice took an edge. Time was running out. He still didn't understand the root of the situation before him. "Why?"

"I can only guess."

"Then guess."

Bustan replied in a tight voice, barely a whisper. "To be sold on."

Black said nothing. The implications were staggering. It took him five seconds to adjust his thoughts.

"And now Remus only wants children?" He nodded at the man and woman to his side. "Their children?"

Bustan didn't answer. He didn't need to. Aksoy answered for him. "Yes. Four kids were taken about a half-hour ago."

Black could barely comprehend the horror. "And do the parents know?"

Again, Aksoy responded. "They know nothing. They don't speak any English. They think they'll be meeting later. I swear, this has nothing to do with me."

"Let me guess," Black said. "You only interpret." He switched to Bustan. "And you were going to get rid of them. That's not very welcoming. Which hospital?"

Bustan responded, voice quiet and fearful. "On the coast I think. Near Troon. Who *are* you? Did Remus send you?"

"Not quite. Deborah Gallagher sent me. In a manner of speaking. She's the woman you sent Ringo to kill. Ringo passes on his regards."

Bustan's mouth dropped. He said nothing.

Lost for words, thought Black. Bad day at the office. Tough shit. Black spoke. "Remus ordered you to arrange her death?"

Bustan nodded.

"I understand. Phone them."

"What?"

"Phone them. Tell them there's two more kids to be picked up. Tell them there was a fuck-up. Six kids, not four. Two were delayed."

"But this has never happened," stammered Bustan. "Why am I doing this?"

Black took a step towards them, and spoke quietly. "Because I'm holding a Beretta semi-automatic pistol aimed at your head, and I'll kill you if you don't do as I ask."

Bustan grabbed his phone lying on the kitchen table, swiped the screen, pressed the keypad.

Black waited, and wondered which level of Hell he had stumbled into.

42

Jason Drummond was in his office, ready. On hand. Timing was everything, and if there were delays, then it was on him. He was head of hospital security. He was the man who made sure events ran smoothly. He was the man who made things happen, who made problems disappear.

So far, so good. The SUV had picked up the kids bang on time, the driver reporting in. No issues. Four kids, as Bustan had promised. The SUV would take fifty minutes to drive from the flat in Govanhill to the hospital, keeping a measured speed, and taking account of traffic lights and road works. The driver reported in every ten minutes, which was normal routine. This particular transportation was new ground for Drummond. Kids only. No parents. No calming reassurance from Mum and Dad. Moods were unpredictable. Crying, screaming. Tantrums. The last thing he needed was a scene.

But so far, so good. According to the driver, two of them were asleep. The other two – the older children – were quiet, subdued almost. Which was perfect.

The arrival time was in fifteen minutes. The SUV would drive through the main entrance, past the front car park, and round the main body of the hospital, then along a single narrow road, to a separate building a mile to the rear, shrouded in trees and foliage, almost invisible to the casual observer. Where Drummond had his office. Where he would meet the new arrivals with a friendly smile, and escort them to a waiting room. There he would stay with them, until a doctor came, also with a friendly smile. Little was ever said, because of the language barrier. But that hardly mattered. Hospitals were to be trusted. Doctors were to be trusted. Life was good. They gladly gave themselves up, because they felt safe and wonderfully free.

They would leave the waiting room, thanking, grateful, and Drummond would never see them again. Alive. The way Drummond saw it, they would have died anyway, in whichever shithole they'd fled from. At least good came out of it, by way of Drummond's bank balance increasing sizeably in bonus money. So, not all bad. In fact, all good.

His thoughts were interrupted by a call on the cheap prepaid burner acquired for the evening, placed on his desktop. Bustan was calling. Which had never happened before. Not after the pick-up. Which meant problems. Attached to the phone, a portable matchbox-sized gadget able to transform his voice into an unrecognisable brassy tone. He answered.

"Yes?"

Bustan's voice. He sounded different. A tremor of excitement, perhaps. "I have two more."

"What?"

A pause. Then Bustan spoke, hesitant. "I hadn't realised. There were six kids. Not four. Two came in separate transport. A mix-up at my end."

Now it was Drummond's turn to pause. A bizarre turn of events. Bustan, up until then, had proved skilled in his organisational abilities. *He hadn't realised.*

"How could this happen?"

"Paperwork got mixed up. The boat captain told us two adults and four children. When six came on board, he didn't tell me. When they arrived on shore, no one bothered to check."

His voice was different, thought Drummond. Not the smug, self-assured Bustan he knew. His voice sounded scared. And Drummond was damned sure he knew why. Bustan had fucked up. He'd made a mistake, and didn't know how the Remus Syndicate would react.

"What will I do with them?" Bustan asked.

Drummond's mind whirled. Six instead of four. Waste not, want not. An extra two items meant a bigger cash bonus. More cash for everyone. It was a win-win situation, and as such, an easy decision. Still, he had a call to make.

"We'll get back."

Drummond disconnected. He took out a mobile from his inside jacket pocket, tapped the keypad. A voice answered. Clipped. Educated. Bordering on formal. His boss. Dr Michael Stapleton.

"Drummond?"

"Bustan says he's got two more kids."

Stapleton replied in less than a heartbeat. "What are you waiting for?"

Drummond called Bustan back, using the burner, using the voice modulator. "We'll come and get them. Forty minutes. And the parents?"

"It will be taken care of. I promise."

"I don't know what a fucking promise means, coming from you. Have them ready."

The call ended. He immediately phoned a second driver, stationed at the hospital. Used should an emergency arise with the first vehicle, such as a flat tyre, or a bad battery, or anything at all.

The command was simple. "Get to the flat. Pick up another two."

Drummond sat back, and gazed at the opposite wall, blank except for the clock and the large wall planner calendar. It was turning out to be a profitable evening. But yet... Something niggled, but he couldn't size it down. He brushed it to one side, and thought rather of the money, and the future, and how it all seemed to glow.

43

"They're coming," said Bustan. He blinked away sweat dribbling into his eyes. "Forty minutes. What are you going to do?"

Black ignored him, turned his attention to the thin figure of Aksoy.

"Tell these people that Bustan has deceived them. That Bustan intended to murder them."

Aksoy, with the Beretta pointing at his chest, became suddenly energetic, directed his full attention to the man and woman, launched into dialogue. Their expressions changed – a mixture of emotion. Their bright new future had vanished. In its place, a nightmare barely believable.

"Tell them their children are in grave danger. Tell them I plan to help them, if I can. Tell them the police can't help." Which was true. The police wouldn't race to a hospital, guns blazing, on the word of illegal immigrants who couldn't speak English. There was procedure. Due protocol. Interviews, reports, requests, decisions, warrants. A whole gamut of arrangements to be put in place, layers of bureaucracy to unpeel, before the Law stirred a muscle. By which time, it was too late.

Suddenly, the woman clutched her husband, sank to her knees. Her husband spoke. The language didn't matter. Fear was distinct, coating every syllable.

Aksoy listened, turned to Black. "He asks what will happen to them."

"I'll get them back," replied Black. He chose not to elaborate. If his suspicions were true, he could never bring himself to articulate such horror to the parents. "Take them back into the living room. Stay with them. I'll be through shortly. Bustan and I need to chat. Don't try to leave. If you do, I'll kill you. You understand me, Aksoy?"

Aksoy's head wobbled up and down, like a puppet's, guided by an invisible thread. "I will not leave. I swear." He helped the woman to her feet, ushered them into the room.

The woman glanced back. "Please," she whispered.

He knew she didn't understand his words, but he answered her anyway. "I'll get them. Whatever it takes."

44

Black gestured Bustan to sit at the kitchen table. Black sat opposite, pistol absently pointed in the vicinity of Bustan's upper chest.

"What happens when your friends arrive?"

Bustan's voice rose to a wheedling plea. "They're not my friends. They forced me to do this. What choice did I have?"

"They forced you? How does that work?"

Bustan's mouth opened, shut. He blew through his lips, blinked again.

"If you're going to talk bullshit," said Black, "you have to be a little quicker on your feet. I'll repeat the question. If you don't answer, I'll shoot you in the throat."

Bustan stared, attention fully focused.

"What happens when your friends arrive?"

"An SUV parks outside. I get a text. One of my men goes out to meet it, to check everything's clear, then they get taken downstairs and go into the car."

"Nice and simple. How long have you been doing this for, Bustan? You don't need to be exact. I'm happy with a guesstimate."

"Not long, I swear!"

Black pursed his lips, furrowed his eyebrows, as if perplexed. "You and your skinny buddy, Aksoy, keep telling me 'you swear'. What do you swear on – the Bible? The Quran? I don't understand. You're a lying piece of shit, so I don't get this 'swear' thing. The way I see it, you've been selling families to this 'hospital' for some time. Months, I reckon. You have a system. You're well organised. This isn't a new bag for you. What do you get – a cash payment per human? A cut of the profits? Trifle with me, Bustan. I'm in a talkative mood."

Bustan licked his lips, formulating his response. The bulge of his Adam's apple shifted up, down as he swallowed. His eyes glistened, Black noted. With tears. Unlike his dead friends in the corridor, Bustan was a man who was very definitely scared of dying.

Black continued. "I think you're a 'cash on delivery' man. You couldn't risk a slice of the profits, because you probably don't know what the profits are. Too easy to be swindled. And you look like a man who would rather swindle, than be swindled. So I'll go for a lump sum of crisp bank notes per head. Would I be right?"

Bustan's chin wobbled. He was on the verge of crying.

"How much do you get?"

Suddenly, Bustan's face changed, from terror to possible salvation. He glimpsed hope, thought Black, where none existed.

"Is it about the money? You want a piece? Of course. I can do this. How much? I can give you £50,000. Just for this one night. We can come to an arrangement. £50,000 each time." He gave a trembling laugh. "You'll become a rich man, yes?"

"Each time?"

"Sure. Every month. No problem. Cash."

"One family every month?"

Bustan talked freely. The terror had diminished. He clearly thought he was onto something.

"Guaranteed. Easy money. It runs like clockwork."

"Except I'm here."

Bustan raised his shoulders as if, *what will be, will be.* "But I see you're a man who knows a good thing when he sees it."

"And the parents? Why kill them? It seems a waste."

Bustan leaned forward a fraction, as if he were conspiring. "They don't want adults anymore. So I was told. More chance of the goods being spoilt. Everything has to be fresh." He smiled, revealing a row of nicotine-stained teeth. "You wouldn't buy rotten fruit from the supermarket."

Black smiled back, like a wolf. "No one likes rotten fruit, Bustan. And Deborah Gallagher?"

Bustan frowned. "I don't know. They told me to arrange her... demise. I follow their orders. Did you kill Ringo? I have no trouble with that. He was always no good. You made him talk, yes? And you came here. You can smell the money, my friend."

Black gave Bustan a level stare. "I'm not your friend. You promise innocent vulnerable people hope. Safety. But all you give them is death. For money. It has to end, Bustan. And it will end. Now. I've made it a mission over the last while to rid the world of evil men. And I'm finding that I rather enjoy it. You're no exception."

Bustan raised a hand, eyes blinking, face a mixture of terror and bewilderment. *He can't comprehend the situation he finds himself in*, thought Black. "Death is easy in the abstract," he said softly. "Not so easy to deal with when faced with the real thing."

Black shot him the face once, twice for good measure.

The impact sent Bustan back, off the chair, onto the floor. Black stood, regarded the lifeless – and featureless – body. A productive night so far.

And the night wasn't over.

45

Dr Percy Canning chose never to wear a surgical gown when he met the intakes. In his mind, people might regard such a sight as unnerving. No one wanted fear and reluctance. Calm and compliance. Far better to work with. Especially with children. He had jeans on, a Levi T-shirt, a pair of white tennis shoes, the most subtle of cologne. He was handsome in a delicate, almost feminine way, and as such, people found him appealing.

With his white winning smile, his smooth tanned skin, his dark perfectly groomed hair, his easy sense of style, he was a living breathing magnet, drawing those he met close. Everybody desired to be his friend. Which was why Michael Stapleton had told him to do it – to meet the intakes. Canning could turn the charm on, like the flick of a switch.

No one wanted fear and reluctance.

Calm and compliance.

Canning met them in the outbuilding at the rear of the hospital grounds. There were two floors. The upper floor housed a number of rooms and offices, where head of security, Jason Drummond, and five men were stationed. Security in this line of work had to be tight, and if required, instant. The ground floor was a waiting room, a prep room, and two theatres. The waiting room was light and modern. Carpets, padded chairs, clean white walls. Music played, just on the periphery of the senses. Classical. Stapleton's choice. Canning hated it. He would have preferred heavy rock, but conceded it wouldn't be conducive to happy and calm.

There were four children. Two were stretched out, asleep. The other two – the older ones – were sitting quietly, not talking. Faces pale and still. Subdued. Trying to take it all in, thought Canning. He'd seen it many times before. That shell-shocked look. Kids bundled away from a war-torn country, travelling hidden in the backs of lorries through Iran, Greece, Italy, France. Then hunched amongst cargo on a boat sailing in the thick of night across the channel. Then here. To the hospital. To this waiting room. A journey like no other. And now they were about to embark on another journey of sorts, and one which they could never have imagined.

Such thoughts ran through Cannings mind for all of a millisecond. Bottom line, he didn't give a shit. Life was a bitch. It was just bad luck. For them. For Drs Canning and Stapleton it was all good, each child representing huge money. Canning gave his splendid smile and thought, *That one will buy me a new Porsche: that one will buy me a new wrap-around extension; and the little ones sleeping softly might, combined, get me a nice house on the Gold Coast. And most importantly, a fucking wagon load of cocaine.*

Canning couldn't speak their language, but that didn't matter. Kids knew a universal language. In one hand he held a bag. He knelt down before them, still smiling, and took out presents, wrapped up in shiny gold paper with red bows.

"For you," he said. He handed one each to the older kids, who at first were hesitant, frowning. They had forgotten such simple gestures. They took them, faces suddenly alive with little smiles. They pulled open the paper. They each had a brand-new Barbie doll, still in its box, looking pristine and perfect. The smiles got bigger. They were happy. Canning was their new friend.

The working unit had to be as small and tight as possible, for obvious reasons. Two theatres, separated by simple white plastic curtains, Stapleton working at one side, Canning the other. Timing was crucial. Dissection had to be swift.

Once the body was suitably hollowed, the removed organs were flushed with oxygen and nutrients, and placed in supercooled containers. Nothing was wasted. Heart, liver, lungs, kidneys, intestines, thymus. Plus corneas, tendons, nerves and veins. Altogether, two hours' work. Solid. Removing was much easier than inserting. But then, thought Canning, that was someone else's problem.

Then the containers had to be moved, which was where they depended on Drummond's organisational qualities. Organs could last up to three days in supercooled conditions, theoretically. Neither Canning nor Stapleton liked to rely on theory. The containers were taken to Prestwick Airport – a matter of twenty-five minutes by car – where they were carefully placed in a secure holder of a private plane owned by the Syndicate. And then away, to their Chinese friends.

The carcasses were disposed of without fuss, bundled into a medical incinerator at the back of the building. All signs of existence gone.

"Thank you," said one of the girls, clutching the Barbie to her chest. She wouldn't be older than ten, thought Canning.

"You're very welcome. Can you help me with your brothers?" He knew she didn't understand, but hoped she would follow by example. He gently picked up one of the little boys. She nodded, picked up the other. With the boy sleeping in his arms, he led her and her sister to the prep room. They followed, willingly, without fuss. They always did.

The prep room had a row of beds. At the side of each bed, a cabinet, upon which was a bottle of water, a glass, a reading lamp, a magazine. They couldn't read English, but that didn't matter. The purpose was to put them at ease – that the whole thing was routine. The procedure was simple and workable. Each intake was given a general anaesthetic, rendering them unconscious within a minute. Under normal circumstances, carried out under the watchful eye of an anaesthetist.

The circumstances were not normal. Canning carried out the anaesthetic himself, feeding a cannula into a vein on the back of their hands, allowing the Isoflurane to do its work. They were then stripped, lifted to a trolley bed, and wheeled to the next room, where Stapleton waited with his long tray of cutting instruments.

Then it began.

One of the girls glanced at Canning, gave a small bashful smile. Canning beamed a smile back. *Don't worry about a thing. All is good in the world.*

Especially good. In Canning's world. The only world that counted.

46

Black left the body of Bustan where it lay, retrieved his mobile, and went back through to the lounge. They would have heard the gunshots, killing Bustan. The man and woman were sitting together on a couch, clutching hands. When Black entered, they regarded him with fearful eyes. No wonder. He'd known them less than thirty minutes, and he'd killed four men. The interpreter – Aksoy – was sitting on a chair opposite. He jumped when the door opened. His eyes darted from Black to the pistol Black was holding.

"You're right," Black said. "Bustan won't be paying you this evening. Nor indeed ever again."

Aksoy nodded. "I understand."

"You're learning fast. The police will be here soon. Gunshots and screams don't go unnoticed. You'll tell them what was happening here. You'll speak for these people."

"You don't have to worry about the police," replied Aksoy.

Black said nothing.

"Because," continued Aksoy, "Bustan owns the block. The flats on either side, and below. No one lives in them. He arranged it that way, in case there should be trouble…" Aksoy faltered, said, "…like this."

"Smart. The money he made from Remus outweighed the hit he took on empty flats. But he won't care about such matters now." Black sat on another chair, the pistol resting on his lap. The man and woman stared at him. "Tell them I intend to find their children."

Aksoy immediately translated.

"Tell them I'll die trying." Aksoy turned him a curious look, as if to say, *You're serious?*

Black was serious, and Aksoy knew it. He translated.

The woman buried her face in her hands, her shoulders shook.

Welcome to Bustan's world, thought Black. *Welcome to paradise.*

"You'll stay with them, Aksoy, until I return with their children. Reassure them."

"And if you don't return?"

Black said nothing.

"What happens then? Once you return?"

"Then you go your way." Black's voice lowered. "But meantime you stay with them. If you leave them before I get back, I'll hunt you down and I'll kill you. If you call any of Bustan's gang, I'll kill you. In fact, if you do anything other than give these people some comfort, I'll kill you. That's the deal. This is your lucky night, Aksoy. You don't get to die, unlike all your friends. Do you understand what I'm saying?"

"Completely."

"Excellent."

Black was dog-tired. Long night. With a bit to go yet. He sat back. The view from where he sat, looking out through the bay windows, was bleak. The opposite tenement block, aglow with the sickly orange shimmer from the street lamps, the night sky a blanket of low cloud. His thoughts drifted to a student's room in

Aberdeen, of a pretty young girl dying in his arms. And inevitably, to another scene, years back. Cradling his murdered daughter and wife, soaked in their blood. His fault. All his fault.

Death was never far from Adam Black.

He adjusted his thoughts.

He *was* death.

They sat in silence. Black was aware all eyes were fixed on him. Probably wondering what the hell he was going to do next. He didn't quite know himself. *Keep moving. Bring the war to them.* Bring chaos to the world of his enemies. It was hardly a structured plan, but it was all he had.

Bustan's phone suddenly pinged. Black swiped the screen.

I'm outside.

Black allowed himself a cold smile.

Game on.

47

Prior to Black firing two bullets in his head, Bustan had described the protocol when the transport arrived. One of his men would meet the car, confirm all was in order, then go back in and get the family. Relatively straightforward. This time however, Black intended to implement certain changes.

He made his way downstairs, and out the building. He was armed with a Beretta, plus two knives he had taken from his assailants. The machete was too awkward to carry, otherwise it would have been useful. When it came to weapons, Black preferred more than less.

A vehicle was stationary on the road, parallel to the parked cars, engine running. A black Mercedes people carrier. Hovering like a shark. The windows were tinted. Impossible to see inside. Black was wearing a dark leather bomber jacket. He pulled up the collar, hunched forward, his face shrouded in shadow. He approached the passenger's side of the car. The window slid down. A single occupant. The driver. A man about thirtyish. Square-shouldered. Deep chest. Dressed in a grey suit, grey tie, sharp white shirt. Crisp, well-shaped features. Gleaming white teeth. He leaned across, squinted up at Black.

"You're new. You guys. A new face every time. No problems here. Get the kids. Don't fuck about."

Black nodded. "Wouldn't dream of it." The Beretta was tucked in his belt. He pulled it out, pointed it at the man's face, the space between the muzzle and the centre of his eyes all of two feet.

The man remained perfectly still. As if he was caught on freeze-frame. He was staring directly at the barrel of a semi-automatic. A twitch of Black's finger, and his head would be spattered on the dashboard.

Black opened the door, sat in the passenger's seat. The man's cologne dominated the senses. The interior looked like it was kept scrupulously clean. Probably for two reasons: to impress the new arrivals, and to keep evidence to a minimum.

"Change of plan," said Black, closing the door behind him.

The man had both his hands resting on the steering wheel. Thick fingered, broad palmed. He exuded experience and lethal expertise. The Remus Syndicate didn't take chances. Black reached over, still pointing the pistol at the man's head, and carefully removed a Mauser 9mm from a shoulder holster set discreetly under his jacket.

"Who the hell are *you*?" There was no fear in the man's voice. No sense of jeopardy. Like the three Turks he had dispatched in the flat. Men of violence. Black knew the measure of the man beside him. No pleading or sobbing. Instead, his brain would be calculating, weighing matters up, waiting. Waiting until the moment was right. Which is exactly what Black would do.

"Let's drive," said Black. "Nice and easy. I don't want to get car sick."

The car glided off, the man giving Black darting glances every few seconds.

"You're in the wrong place, pal. Wrong fucking place, wrong fucking time."

"I'm not your pal. Keep driving."

"Where are we going?"

"To the hospital."

The man gave a humourless laugh. "Jesus. What are you? You're not a cop. Some sort of fucking gung-ho vigilante? Let it go. You're way over your head. What do you say I drop you off right now, and you disappear, and we never meet again. This is good advice, pal."

"There are two things you have to understand. One. I'm really not your pal. Maybe this is a boy scout thing, or you were a lonely child. But you have to understand that a man pointing a pistol at your head is not your pal. Or perhaps you're stupid. Two. I want you to give me the name of the hospital you're going to, and then take me to it. This is more than a polite request. It's a demand."

The man stayed silent for a space of several seconds, then said, "What hospital? You need a doctor?"

Black had been anticipating such a response. "Not me." He pulled out the stiletto blade from his jacket inside pocket, stretched across, and drew it deep down the side of the man's face, from the side of his eye to the corner of his lip. The man shrieked, the car veering to one side. Black pressed the pistol against the man's jacket, next to the ribs. "Easy."

The man straightened the wheel. Blood flowed. Suddenly the interior was not so pristine.

"Are you fucking mad!"

"Possibly. But now I'm hoping I have your full attention. Tell me the name."

Blood was running freely onto the man's white collar, onto his shoulder. Thirty stitches at least. Probably more.

"The Rosewood."

"Not so difficult." Black had never heard of it. Probably one of those neat little boutique hospitals geared round the ailments of ultra-rich people. "Now drive there. And if I find you're lying, I'll not be so pleasant."

The man took a deep breath. Still no fear. Anger. He could feel it. It was as potent as his cologne.

"You don't fucking know what you're getting into."

"I'm sure. What's your name?"

The man didn't respond, eyes fixed ahead.

"It's only polite," continued Black. "And I don't want to cut you again. Shame to get blood stains on these nice leather seats."

"Paul Turner."

"Thank you. My name is Adam Black. What's the procedure? You have to call at specific times? Do they call you?"

"There's no procedure. You're fucking mad. You think this is some fucking James Bond movie?"

Black leaned back against the passenger door, pistol pointed in the direction of the driver's waist. He knew he was lying, but there was little purpose in pursuing the matter. Turner could make anything up, and Black would never know the difference. Black had to assume worst-case scenario. That the hospital would very quickly realise trouble was coming.

He was weary to the core.

"Turn the heating off," he said.

Turner pressed a button on the dashboard. Black needed to stay sharp. The worst was still to come.

"Do you know what happens to them, Turner?"

"What do you mean?"

"The families you transport in your exclusive taxi trip. The children. Do you know what happens to them when they get to the hospital?"

"Don't know what you're talking about."

"Sure you do. But it's not new. If I recall, Hitler organised such excursions back in the day. Though on a much grander scale."

"You're fucking mad. I don't know what you're talking about."

"Do they pay you well, Turner. For what you do?"

"I just drive."

"Sure you do. With a Mauser tucked under your jacket. What's that for? A little target practice if the journey gets boring?"

Turner chose not to respond. He had one hand raised to his face, to staunch the blood. Black couldn't have cared less. They were heading southwest, towards the coast. They had just reached the M77. It was just after 4.45am, and getting lighter, though the dawn sun was still hidden by rain clouds.

The roads were quiet. On either side, tightly packed pine trees, and beyond, the rolling wilderness of the Eaglesham Moors, the skyline littered with insect-like silhouettes. Windmills. Hundreds of them. The governments plan for cheap energy. Such a shame it ruined the landscape. The greater good. Black gave it only a cursory thought. He had weightier things on his mind.

Turner's mobile phone was sitting in the centre console. Suddenly it lit up, its ring tone loud in the car. A number appeared on the main screen. *Checking in. Perhaps wondering what the hell was going on.*

"What shall I do?"

Black wasn't oblivious to Turner's sarcasm. He felt almost impressed. Despite a slash down his face, and sitting on the wrong side of a semi-automatic, he still wasn't afraid.

"Answer it."

"You're the boss."

Turner tapped the screen. A voice immediately spoke, undisguised, unlike the voice during Bustan's conversation.

"Speak, Turner."

Turner cocked his head a fraction at Black, one eyebrow raised. *What shall I say, boss?*

Black responded.

"Turner's concentrating on the road. Thought I might answer for him."

Silence. Black pictured the recipient, sitting at whichever desk he was sitting at, his mind alive with a range of disturbing possibilities.

"My name is Adam Black. Let me tell you where we're at. Bustan and several of his men are dead. I took delight in ending their lives, though I suspect they didn't share that feeling. You can thank me later."

Black paused, letting that sink in, then continued.

"The parents of the children you have are waiting for their return. I'm with Turner right now, who has very kindly offered to drive me to your little factory of death. We should be there soon. Once we arrive, it becomes a very simple arrangement. If the children are handed over, alive and well, then I'll let you live. If they're dead, then I'll kill you and everything around you."

Another silence. Then the phone disconnected.

"Jesus..." Turner muttered. "You have a fucking screw loose. You've told them you're coming. They know you're not a cop. What the fuck do you think's going to happen when you get there? Balloons and banners? A fucking fanfare? You're a fucking dead man, Adam fucking Black."

Turner was right, of course. But it hardly mattered. They would have guessed something was wrong already. If he'd told Turner to make up an excuse, they'd have seen through it in a millisecond. Therefore, do the unexpected. Tell them you're coming, that you're not afraid, and that you're bringing a whole raging shitstorm with you. Get them rattled. Also, and crucially, it might make them think twice about killing the kids, in case they can be used to barter with.

If they were still alive. If they were dead, Black would fulfil his promise, and destroy them all.

Turner hadn't stopped talking. "Who the fuck do you think you are, Black. Fucking Batman? They will hunt you down, my friend, and kill you. Is that what you want? For what? Some nameless kids who don't mean shit to anyone?"

Black kept his voice neutral. "Their mother and father might disagree. You like the movies. Bond and Batman. Both killers in their own way. So maybe your comparison isn't a million miles off. We share something in common."

Turner gave a sneering response. "Which is?"

"We only kill bad guys."

48

Jason Drummond hung up, took five seconds to rationalise what had just happened. Somehow, security had been breached. Bustan had talked. A guy was heading in their direction. He wasn't the police. Related somehow to the kids? Possible, but not probable. Maybe on his own, maybe not. Drummond had to assume not. Sent by someone? Again, possible. A thousand questions, all of which impossible to answer. But he was coming, which meant trouble.

Suddenly, the niggle he'd felt when he'd spoken to Bustan made sense. Bustan had sounded scared. Drummond had assumed it was fear of the Syndicate – Bustan had fucked up, explaining there were two more kids. Drummond should have realised. When he told Bustan they would be picked up, Bustan hadn't asked the golden question, the one he always asked – *How much will I get?*

He phoned Stapleton, who picked up immediately.

"We have a problem. A guy called Adam Black says he's coming to get the kids. Bustan must have talked. Black sounds like he means business. He's in Turner's car. I assume he's forcing Turner to take him here."

Silence, then, "One man?"

"Could be more. Impossible to say. We must assume the worst. I think we should close the operation down, give him the kids, let the whole thing blow over. Maybe start it up in a few months. Start fresh."

Stapleton responded in an icy tone. "I pay you to deal with things like this. And you get extremely well paid, Drummond. Sort it. Do what you're supposed to do. We proceed as normal. Nothing changes. You understand? We stay on course. Now please. I have work to do."

The phone went dead. Drummond clenched his teeth in frustration. This was a bad situation. But Stapleton was right. Drummond got paid well, and he didn't want it to end. He had been given an order. He would therefore follow it through. *Fucking medics*, he thought. *What the hell do they know.*

He got up, left the office, to a common room at the end of the corridor, where four men were waiting. Plus, he had another seven in and around the hospital. He had plans to make, and limited time.

Trouble was coming. Drummond had spent his entire adult life dealing with trouble. His response to it was brutally simple.

Crush it quick.

And who the fuck was Adam Black?

Stapleton seethed with anger, which was not an ideal state of mind prior to a major operation. Anger at his head of security, Jason Drummond, who appeared to have no conception of how things worked. *Start it up in a few months. Start fresh.* They had four items, prepped and ready. Equating to roughly forty million. The Chinese paid, and paid well. They expected results. Even the suggestion of delay was inconceivable. They would simply go elsewhere. Another hospital, another country. It was naïve to think The Remus Syndicate were the only suppliers.

The operations would proceed, exactly as planned. The children were in the prep room, Canning ready to administer the anaesthetic.

He would let Drummond do his job, and deal with this upstart. This man called Adam Black.

49

Little was said in the car. Turner's shoulder was saturated with blood.

"I need to get to a hospital," Turner said. The irony wasn't lost on Black.

"Lucky you. We're going to the right place."

They took the M77 for a further twenty-five minutes, keeping the speed at a steady 60mph. The motorway merged onto the A77. They carried on for another couple of miles. Turner slowed, took a left turn, circled the car up and across a bridge over the main road, heading west towards the village of Dundonald. The road was much narrower, on either side trees and thick foliage. No street lights.

"How far?" Black asked.

"Five miles."

The road dipped and twisted. Two miles later they got to the village of Dundonald, comprising little more than a pub, a couple of shops, and a row of old terraced built houses on either side of the street. The place was deserted. In the distance, an outline of a ruined castle. In the early pre-dawn stillness, the place had a surreal witchy quality. They passed through, and back into the country. They passed a sign for Troon – eight miles.

They took another sharp turn, up a single lane road with passing points every two hundred yards or so. Woodland on either side. Turner had the car lights on full beam. After five minutes, a plaque on a cairn style rockery, beside a road cutting to the right, leading into the gloom of trees – **ROSEWOOD HOSPITAL.**

"Pull in," said Black.

Turner obeyed, pulling the people carrier onto a grass verge on the side of the road. He turned to Black. The side of Turner's face was a mess.

"Tell me about the layout of the hospital," Black said. "Please."

"What then, Black? You plan on killing me? In my book, that's murder."

Black said nothing. He took the car keys, placed them in his jacket pocket. He got out of the car, went round to the driver's side, gestured Turner to get out. Slowly, with deliberation, Turner opened the car door, swivelled round, putting his feet on the grass. Black took two steps back, kept his pistol aimed at Turner's chest. Turner got out, faced Black, one hand still clutching his face, the other placed behind his back.

"I won't kill you, Turner, if you co-operate. Tell me the layout of the hospital. I won't ask again."

Turner gave a small shrug. "The road goes up about a half mile, through the woods. The hospital owns all the grounds. You'll get to a car park, in front of the main building. Follow the road round, past the hospital, and drive for another mile, to a smaller building. That's where they go. That's all I can tell you. What now, Black? What's the game plan?" He raised the hand holding his face into the air, palm and fingers smeared in blood.

"Look at me. I need to get this seen to." He stepped towards Black, still talking.

Turner suddenly crouched, brought his other hand round, aiming a pistol. Black was prepared. Turner's movements had been designed to distract. He had accessed another weapon, secreted under the driver's seat.

Black fired once, into Turner's chest. Turner bounced back onto the car. Black approached, fired again, a head shot, slicing away the top section of Turner's skull. For a second, Turner seemed suspended, some vestigial brain power keeping him on his feet, his face slack and blank. Life departed. He slithered to the ground.

Black shot him again, where he lay, for good measure. Better too much, than too little. He placed his pistol in his pocket, opened the rear door of the car, heaved Turner up, and bundled him onto the rear seat directly behind the driver's. He straightened him, tucked his legs in, fastened the seat belt round him. Turner's head lolled to one side, his face scarred and ghoulish. Black patted him on the cheek. Turner could still be useful.

A half-mile to the hospital, then a further mile beyond.

Clock was ticking. They knew Black was coming. Which was fine. There was no other way. This was never going to be a subtle situation. Children's lives were in the balance, and as such, any measure of restraint was dispensed with.

This was "shock and awe". And if the kids were dead, Black would burn them all.

Black got in the car, started the engine, turned and drove up the wooded entrance.

Hell was coming to breakfast.

50

The four children were unconscious, lying on trolley beds next to each other, oblivious to the fate that would befall them. They were stripped naked. Canning had put the presents he had given them in a box. They would be used later, for the next batch.

Canning wheeled each trolley, one at a time, into the adjacent room, containing two fully functioning theatres, separated by a plastic curtain on a rail. Canning would work in one. Stapleton, the other.

Stapleton was waiting, masked, adorned in a full surgical gown, standing next to the operating table, where he would perform the dissections and removals. Above, three massive LED circular lighting displays, emitting pure white colour. Around, four colour displays mounted on retractable pendants. Two scrub sinks. Utility columns. On a side unit, neatly arranged, a row of implements: scalpels, scissors, saws, forceps, clamps, chisels. Many others. In the strong glare of the overhead lighting, they glittered.

"You ready?" said Stapleton.

"Let me get changed, and scrubbed up," replied Canning. "Five minutes."

"I'll wait for you."

Canning left the theatre, back to the waiting room, and into a personal changing room, complete with shower. When he worked, he liked to wear a pair of fresh loose-fitting jogging trousers and baggy T-shirt, over which he would wear his surgical gown.

He looked in the mirror. The face looking back was clean-cut, delicate, intelligent. He took out his credit card and a small plastic pouch from his pocket, gently prised open one end, emptied the content on the unit beside the sink, and using the card, arranged it into a neat line, bent, snorted. He gazed again at the mirror, and felt invincible.

He gave his glowing smile. Tonight he'd make a ton of money.

And Canning loved money more than anything else in the world.

Drummond had to make certain assumptions. Worst-case scenarios. That Black was working with others. That Turner had provided him with key information – in particular, the location of the unit at the back of the hospital, where the children were placed. That Turner was dead. That Black would probably leave the car at some relatively close spot, and make his way by foot. Which was the biggest single dilemma. They were positioned in dense woodland, a mile from the main building, miles from anywhere else. Pointless in searching the grounds. Drummond had ten men at his disposal. If they spaced out, and combed the area, it would still be relatively easy for a well-disciplined enemy to creep through the gaps. Better then to adopt a siege mentality.

The building they were in was hidden away, surrounded by trees and bushes. One narrow road in and out. There was a small and exclusive parking bay on one side, big enough for a half-dozen cars. There was a single door at centre front. Heavy glass, with automatic locking system. There was floodlighting on each of the four exterior walls. Normally, they weren't used. Now however, Drummond had them on. Illuminating the area like it was Christmas. There were no windows. The roof was flat, two storeys high, the walls were smooth cladding. Virtually impossible to scale. Even then, once on top, there was nowhere to go.

He grouped his men in simple straightforward positioning. Six men at the front door, and two at each of the front corners. Every man armed with a 9mm Glock 22, holding thirteen rounds. Complete with silencers, for obvious reasons. There were other patients in the main hospital building. Life still went on. If there had to be a firefight, he didn't want panic. Panic brought its own problems. Including cops.

Drummond stayed in the interior, in the lobby between the front entrance and the waiting room. The operating theatres were just down the corridor. If things got bad, then the doctors were only five seconds way, to warn them and get them the hell out. Which was another headache. Drummond had never been happy with the design of the building, with only one exit, and no other means of escape. Stapleton had disagreed. It was secure, unwanted guests couldn't get in, unhappy patients couldn't leave. What could go wrong? He wanted Fort Knox, and he got it. Only trouble was, it was also a trap.

Such were the many thoughts running through Drummond's mind, as he waited, Glock in one hand, radio receiver in another. His men were outside, as ready as they could be. They were trained, ex-military. Hard men.

He took a deep breath, his iron discipline dismissing the

flutter of nerves in his stomach, and for the millionth time, cursed Stapleton for his arrogance. And stupidity. The operation should have been closed down, mothballed until matters settled, and they knew more about their enemy.

Drummond squinted through the front glass door. A beam of light. A voice cracked on the radio.

"There's someone coming."

51

But not all men seek rest and peace; some are born with the spirit of the storm in their blood.
— Anonymous

The single lane to the hospital lacked any lighting. Black put on the full beam. Trees on either side, forming a tunnel of darkness. The road swept round to the left, in one long curve. Turner said it stretched for about a half mile, until it reached the main body of the hospital. Follow it round, and then keep on it for a further mile. Black kept his speed at 30mph. Black expected men stationed at points of the road. He saw no one.

A minute passed. Suddenly, the trees gave way. Before him, an impressive glass cuboidal structure, glittering like a jewelled box bathed in the lights of an adjacent car park. The entrance comprised two wide electric revolving doors. Inside, Black glimpsed a reception area, people at the front desk. The car park was only a quarter full.

All was quiet. No men waiting at the entrance. No one stopping him on the road. They were drawing him in. Black followed the road round, passing the car park on his left, keeping a steady thirty. The road ran parallel to the side of the hospital building. To his right, a garden area, with antique-style metal-framed garden benches, grass trimmed to perfection, neat flower beds. Beyond, a wall of tightly packed trees.

Black drove on. A mile beyond the main building, Turner had said. Black passed the hospital, the road snaking through more gardens, with manicured lawns and bright flowers. The road continued, then entered the darkness of the woods beyond, dipping down, and Black was back to driving through gloom and shadow.

There! Ahead some distance, glinting through the trees, flickers of light. Then gone, as the road twisted. There again! They were waiting for him, ready and prepared. No question of concealment. Daring him. The road turned and twisted. He got to a sharp bend, and now hit a straight road. Before him, about two hundred yards, a small detached building, ablaze with light. A group of men waiting outside. His reception party. He had no doubt they could see him. His headlights were on full beam, and he was in plain sight.

Black swerved the car round. Turning was difficult. The road was narrow, hemmed in on either side by a solid line of trees. Black turned the steering wheel this way, that. A three-point turn turned into a five-point turn, branches scraping front and back. The body work would need a respray. He faced the opposite direction. He pulled the seat back as far as possible, hunkered down, stretching his legs, his head almost below the window. He adjusted the rear-view mirror. He moved the gear stick to reverse, started the car moving, keeping the vehicle steady.

"Keep it cool, Turner." Of course, Turner would never

answer, because Turner was dead. But he could still prove useful. Black reckoned the shooting would start at around a hundred yards. Maybe more, if they had rifles, and with the right ones, they would start shooting now. The car was a seven-seater people carrier. A bullet would have to pass through the back exterior, then the back seat, then the middle seat where Turner sat, then through Turner, then the driver's seat. A lot of substance. Enough, hopefully, to dampen the impact. If specialist ammunition was used, then the car, and Turner, and ultimately Black, would be cut in half.

He pressed two buttons on the centre console. His window, and the passenger's window, slid down. The Mauser taken from Turner rested in the compartment by the gear stick, next to Black's left hand. The Beretta was in the side compartment in the driver's door, to his right. He had two hunting knives tucked under his jacket.

He was more a weapon than a man.

Black pressed his foot on the accelerator, keeping both hands locked on the steering wheel, eyes fixed on the rear-view mirror, single-minded as a shark. He was coming fast. Fifty, sixty, seventy miles per hour. The men at the front door were shouting, assuming classic shooting stances – feet, shoulder width apart, two-handed grip, arms straight, locked elbows.

Black braced himself. The bullets started, knocking through the car, little plinks of noise, sounding as innocent as someone tapping metal with the tips of their fingers to the beat of some crazy jazz tune. Suddenly, the rear window shattered. The car juddered. A bullet ripped through the car seat, six inches above Black's head, cracking the front windscreen. Others followed. The front windscreen disintegrated. Bullets rippled through the interior. Black felt the vibration of Turner's body, absorbing the impact. Fifty yards. The men abandoned their pistol stance, rushing to either side to avoid being crushed.

Ten yards. Black curled into a ball, and waited for impact.

Canning left the changing room, properly attired in his dark green surgical gown, gloves, mask. Embroidered in red stitching on the right shoulder, his initials – PC. A theatrical touch, but what was the harm? He'd slept well the night before, plus he'd caught a catnap around 10pm. He felt good. He felt sharp. Sleep was important in his line of work. One weary slip, an organ nicked by a careless scalpel, and suddenly the profits were down.

Stapleton was waiting for him. Beside him, the four trolley beds, each occupied by a sleeping child, all in a line. An orderly queue, thought Canning. Waiting peacefully to be dissected.

"You took your time," said Stapleton. His voice was terse. Canning sensed tension, which was unusual.

"What's the problem? I'm here." He glanced at the Rolex sparkling on his wrist. "We've got eight hours. Is something wrong?"

Stapleton shook his head. "Let's crack on." Stapleton wheeled up the nearest trolley parallel to the operating table. On it, the girl Canning had given the Barbie doll to. The girl was on her back, face pale and softened by deep sleep, her naked body covered by a thin sheet. Canning took her legs, Stapleton her shoulders. Deftly, they transferred her to the table. Without speaking, Canning pushed the next trolley, carrying one of the little boys, across the room, through the opened curtains to the adjacent theatre. Stapleton followed, silent. Canning wondered. Stapleton was usually chatty. Excited. He seemed muted. On edge.

They repeated the process, transferring the boy.

"Let's get started," said Stapleton.

"Of course."

Canning returned to his own operating table. There, before him, the girl. He never knew their names. He didn't care, particularly. Next to the bed, a plastic shelf clamped to a pendant, and on the shelf, a long tray. On the tray, a neat row of cutting implements. All shapes and sizes. The process began with a neat slit from just below the centre of the collarbone, down to the navel. Then opening the body. *Like finding a treasure trove*, he thought.

He looked at her. A perfect body. Full of health and promise. About to be split and sent to faraway places.

His hand hovered above the tray. He picked up a short-handled scalpel. He leaned over, touched the tip of the blade gently on her skin, got ready to press.

And then the world exploded.

52

The entrance to the building was glass. Drummond watched the drama unfold from his position in the lobby. He saw the headlights. He watched the car manoeuvre a tight turn on the road. Now he saw its tail lights. He watched as it gained speed toward them.

"Mad fucker," he muttered. So much for his prediction of a clandestine attack through the woods. He clicked the radio receiver. "Kill the bastard."

He saw his men assumes firing stances. *Should have fucking rifles.* The place was virtually soundproofed. He couldn't hear the noise of the pistols discharging, but he saw the recoil, and knew they were firing. The vehicle was gaining speed, undeterred. *One clean head shot, and it was over.* But it kept coming.

He dropped the receiver, aimed his pistol, waited, thinking *Somebody stop this fucker.*

But the fucker kept coming.

~

Black was close enough to take his hands off the wheel, and with a gun in each hand, started firing to his left and right, through the open windows of the car. He was moving at high speed, firing indiscriminately. Accuracy was impossible. Luck more than skill. Luck prevailed. There were two groups of men on either side, forced to dodge away last second. Black glimpsed their disbelieving faces. Three crumpled to the ground. Whether dead or merely wounded, Black didn't know. Nor did he have time to care.

The car rammed through the front of the building, the door and surrounding wall bursting away, then through a main pillar, bringing down the ceiling, until it slammed hard up against the back wall, battered and crushed.

Black thrust open the driver's door. Dust billowed. Sparks and flashes. Twisted spikes of steel hung broken, like dismembered limbs. The place groaned and creaked, as concrete shifted, as load-bearing walls suddenly ceased to bear the load.

Black stumbled from the car. He saw shapes creep through the great ragged space where the door had been. *Keep moving.* He crouched, took a second to orientate his senses, picked his way forward, careful with his step. Suddenly, a great surge of noise. Another portion of the ceiling collapsed, raining lumps of concrete and iron, stirring up more dust cloud. Men screamed.

Black leapt to the ground, waited, breath held. He moved forward again, crawling on his belly, inch by inch. Three more shapes appeared. The place echoed to the distinctive sound of gunshots, as they fired at the car. They hadn't seen Black. Black aimed, fired, three pops. Three figures dropped to the ground, falling within a second of each other, dead before they knew it.

Black waited. A stillness settled. The remaining men – if there were any – wouldn't dare enter. Easy targets. So Black hoped. He rose to his feet, made his way further into the building. The car had ended in a room with chairs and drinks machines. Like a waiting room. Only now the chairs and drinks machines were smashed to hell and back. The room was open plan into a broad corridor. Doors on either side. The lighting flickered. Rubble drizzled down. He was walking in a nightmare. Of his own making, he thought grimly.

A door opened at the far end. A man appeared. Dark suit, coated in a fine mesh of dust. In his hand, a gun. Looked like a Browning.

"My name is Jason Drummond!" he shouted. "Let's talk."

When Drummond realised the car was not for stopping, he ran. Primarily to avoid being crushed, but also to get to his paymasters, warn them, and somehow get them the hell out. He sprinted down the corridor. The building shuddered. The car hurtled through, like a great beast, amid a roar of destruction. Door, walls, ceiling – the world was a sudden mad whirl of glass and metal and concrete. Drummond didn't stop.

He got to the door of the operating room, barged in. There, standing poised over an unconscious child, was Percy Canning, one hand clasping a scalpel. He stared at Drummond. He pulled the mask from his face, his delicate features a mixture of fear and bewilderment. The plastic curtain swept aside, and Stapleton stood, hands on his hips. His gaze burned into Drummond. No fear or shock there. Unbridled fury.

He spoke, his voice rising to a pitch. "What the fuck's happening!"

"It's Adam Black," replied Drummond. "He's crashed a car into the building."

"Adam who?" It was Canning who spoke, turning to

Stapleton. Stapleton ignored him, maintaining his focus on Drummond.

"Why aren't you fucking dealing with this!"

"I wasn't expecting..." Drummond searched for the right words, "...such a direct assault."

"Do I look as if I give a fuck?"

"Adam who?" repeated Canning.

The trolleys shook, the equipment rattled on their fixed pendants. A sound like grinding steel emanated from the walls. Then a crash. More ceiling had collapsed, Drummond assumed.

"We can get out of this." Drummond tried to keep his voice calm. "This guy, Black, he only wants the kids. We give them up, then he's gone. It's all he cares about."

Stapleton took a deep breath, chest puffing up. "Do you think I'm going to give up a fortune just because one fucking jumped up scrapper comes knocking at our door."

"He's hardly knocking," Canning said.

Stapleton turned him a leaden gaze, then resumed back to Drummond.

"Offer him money. Go out, and tell him I can transfer a million from the Remus account into whatever account he wants, anywhere. I can do this now, from my mobile phone. He can have the money in thirty seconds."

"And then what?"

"Then we deal with it. With him. We find him, and kill the fucker. But that's for later. We'll pay him off."

"It won't work," Drummond said. "Not with this guy. He thinks he's a hero. You can't negotiate with a man like Black. There's no common ground. It's all or nothing."

"And when did you become a fucking psychoanalyst?" snarled Stapleton. "Everyone has their price. Now go and do your fucking job!"

Drummond said nothing. There was nowhere to go. Black

was in the building, doubtless carrying formidable fire power. With all the carnage, Drummond's men would find it difficult, if not impossible, to catch him as a target. The only way out was back through the now destroyed front entrance. Which meant through Black.

"Men like Black don't have a price," Drummond muttered. He turned, opened the door, and entered the corridor. At the far end, a man was approaching.

Adam Black.

Drummond drew himself up, felt the reassuring touch of the Browning in his right hand.

"My name's Jason Drummond!" he shouted. "Let's talk!"

"Let's," replied Black. He stopped, a distance of about twenty-five yards between them. He considered the man called Jason Drummond. Compact, muscular, capable. Thick neck, wide shoulders. A man, thought Black, exuding that indefinable quality of lethal competence.

Drummond continued. "We can work through this."

"Work through what?"

Drummond made a show of looking around. "This chaos. It doesn't achieve anything."

"It achieves plenty for me."

"You're here for the children. But broaden your horizons, Black. We can come to an arrangement."

"Broaden my horizons? There's an expression. An arrangement?"

Drummond took a step closer, then another, the hand holding the Browning held loosely by his side with a casual innocence, as if it were a mobile phone, or a set of car keys.

"We don't want trouble. We want this to go away. You understand? What could make this go away, Black?"

"I'm out of magic wands. So how about handing over the kids you have. That would be a start."

Drummond gave a cold laugh. "I can tell you're ex-army, yes? The way you move, the way you act. An old soldier. Fighting for queen and country for shit pay and no thanks. Forgotten by the system. I've been there, and didn't like it. Not one bit. Live a little, Black. Perhaps it's time for a bit of payback. Let me tell you now, we can put a million pounds in whatever account you want. You'll be a millionaire before breakfast. Then you go your way, we go ours. You become a rich man. The champagne's on us. Imagine."

"I'm trying to. And what do you get?"

"We get your silence, and you stop your... crusade. Or whatever this is."

"I can see that working out. And the children?"

Drummond had made his way slowly down the corridor, stopped close enough for Black to see the sweat glistening on his forehead.

Drummond responded in a brassy tone. "Fuck them! Who cares about some illegal immigrant kids from some shithole arse-end country. Technically, they don't exist. A million pounds, Black. That's a lot of cash. I'll tell my men to back off. You leave here, and we never see each other again."

Black nodded contemplatively, then spoke. "I served in the Special Air Service. I didn't do it for the money, nor the thanks. I did it because, deep down, I suppose I enjoy killing people. Especially bad people. Call it a personality flaw. Which makes me a rather awkward person to negotiate with."

Drummond blinked away the sweat, opened his mouth to speak, then clamped it shut, clearly at a loss for words. The hand holding the Browning trembled.

"And as for the kids?" continued Black, eyes glittering. "The kids who don't technically exist? They exist in my book. And I'll make damn sure they continue to exist."

He whipped his hand up, shot the man called Jason Drummond once in the upper chest, two inches below the chest, and once in the skull, an inch above the eyes, dead centre in the sweating forehead. Quick succession, two shots morphing into one. Drummond staggered back, took a faltering foot forward, like a drunk catching his balance, sank to his knees, dropped face down onto the floor.

Black stepped round him. "I've never liked champagne."

Drummond had appeared from a door at the far end of the corridor. It seemed the logical place for Black to go.

Stapleton, unlike his friend, Percy Canning, was not scared. He was outraged. An individual had invaded his space, interrupted the money-making process, and worst of all, potentially jeopardised future relations with his Chinese associates, should they ever find out. Which they would. Such a thing was intolerable.

Canning was staring at him, terror plain on his face.

"Who the fuck's Adam Black!" Canning's voice was a shriek.

"He's nothing," snapped Stapleton.

"Nothing! He's just fucking smashed a car into the front door. Now you're offering him a million to disappear. That's some fucking nothing!"

Stapleton turned, gave him a burning look. "You know what this is? A blip. In this game, there's always blips. You think, what we do, we're going to live a trouble-free existence? You think, when you start up the engine on your new Porsche 911, that these things don't come at a price? When you open the fucking door to your three-million-plus London apartment, there's no payback? This is the grit that gets under the nails. Get over it, Percy. Drummond will take care of this, like he takes care of all the blips. Then we move on."

"Move on? To what? Prison? Worse? You haven't answered my question. This is more than just a fucking blip. Who the hell's Adam Black?"

Stapleton deigned not to answer. The truth was, he had no idea. But it didn't matter. Drummond would take care of it. An image flashed in his mind. The picture in the conference room in the main building of the hospital. *Chaos*. Perhaps that was how he should have answered Canning – *This man Adam Black? He's everything I hate. He's the picture on the wall. He is chaos.*

A sound from the corridor outside, distinct and sharp. A gunshot. Maybe two. Canning, beside him, jolted round.

"See?" said Stapleton, a triumphant ring in his voice. "Drummond does what he does. Who's Adam Black? A corpse with a bullet in his skull."

Both men remained still. On the table next to them, an unconscious girl, oblivious to the turmoil around her. The door opened. A man stood, framed against the flickering strip lights outside. In one hand, a pistol.

The man was not Jason Drummond.

Chaos had arrived.

53

The scene Black confronted possessed the surreal quality of a nightmare, and one which would long remain in his memory. A naked girl, no older than ten, lying on an operating table, asleep. To one side of the room, trolleys, a child on each. Two men beside the girl, garbed in surgical gowns. A neat row of cutting blades stretched on a tray. The white glare of lights.

Two fiends, hunched over... what? A human sacrifice, thought Black.

He approached them. Neither was armed. Neither presented danger. One was in his mid-fifties. Sixties perhaps. Smooth tanned complexion. Iron-grey hair, swept back from his forehead, alert lucent eyes. The other was younger. Possibly in his late thirties. Delicate, almost feminine features. Dark hair, trimmed and neat. Also tanned.

The younger one backed off, stumbling into equipment on a unit, knocking it to the ground. He raised his hand, pointed at the older one.

"This was his idea!" he blurted. "We can work this out. No need to point the gun. His name is Stapleton. He's the one responsible!"

The older one didn't move, stared at Black with an unnerving intensity.

Black spoke in a quiet voice, addressing the younger man. "What's your name?"

"Canning. Percy Canning. I'm a heart surgeon."

"What's that in your hand?"

"This?" Canning looked at the scalpel, as if he'd seen it for the first time. "The girl needs surgery. I was..." He dropped the scalpel. If fell to the tiled floors, making a little tinkling sound. He backed further off, then sank to his knees, burying his head in his hands. He began to weep. He spoke in little gasping bursts. "Please. This is not what you think. Don't kill me. I don't want to die."

"Of course you don't." Black shot him in the head, then trained his pistol at the older man.

"Dr Stapleton."

Stapleton displayed no fear of the situation. The reverse. He seemed indignant. Angry. Black was mildly impressed.

"You've just murdered one of the country's leading heart surgeons. In cold blood."

"It was my pleasure. So this is Remus. You and your colleague – sorry, *ex-colleague* – are part of the Remus Syndicate. Interesting set-up. Bustan supplied a constant flow of people no one would ever miss. They were brought here, to this little abattoir. Where you and you chum used your not-insignificant skill to perform some removals. Organ removals, I would imagine. To be sold. To who? The Russians? Chinese?"

"You wouldn't understand."

"No. I wouldn't. I would be surprised if anyone did. But it all kicked off with Desmond Gallagher. A human rights lawyer who uncovered what you and your cabal were up to, and who was about to expose you. So you do what you do, Dr Stapleton. You picked up the phone. You sent a memo. You had him killed."

Stapleton's eyes narrowed. His forehead rippled into tiny, bewildered wrinkles. "Gallagher? You're way off the mark. He was an upstart lawyer who had heard rumours. About us. We threatened him. We sent him warning letters. But we were never really concerned. We never touched him."

Black said nothing.

"But his death was advantageous," continued Stapleton. "Call it luck. One of those remarkable coincidences. It stopped his interference."

"And his wife? You arranged for her to die. Only she didn't. I'd call that bad luck."

Stapleton gave the merest shrug. "My Chinese connections knew about Gallagher, like they know about everything. They wanted matters tidied up, in case Gallagher had revealed information to his wife, which was entirely possible, even though there was little to tell. They assumed we had killed Gallagher. They asked us to finish things off. I agreed. We had to keep relations."

"The Chinese are your paymasters."

"Yes."

Black scrutinised Stapleton, seeking a shred of remorse, but saw nothing.

He said, "You don't really give a shit, do you, Stapleton. Why children?"

Stapleton responded with a careless flick of his fingers, as if removing a speck of dust from his sleeve. He spoke in an indifferent manner. "They're cleaner. Less chance of corruption. The organs are, generally, pristine."

"Pristine. Nice turn of phrase. They're human beings."

"They're commodities."

"They might offer a different opinion."

"It's a matter of perspective. We can still come to an arrangement. Drummond said one million. What if I said two million. Transferred to your account. I merely press some digits on my mobile phone. You leave a wealthy man."

"Money doesn't interest me."

"Then what do you want?"

"How about a neat conclusion."

Stapleton tilted his head back, regarded Black with a glittering gaze.

"This doesn't go away. The Chinese will find a new hospital. New doctors. A new supply. What have you achieved?"

"Closure."

"Not quite." The girl lay flat on the operating table before Stapleton. The tray of surgical equipment was at his elbow. He snatched up a small, hooked blade, and pressed it to the girl's neck. "This is how this plays out, Black. If you so much as twitch, I'll slice her throat before..."

He never finished the sentence. The act of cutting the girl's throat – the pressure of the hand, the turn of the wrist, the movement of the arm – could never outmatch the split second it took Black to squeeze the trigger and the subsequent time for the bullet to travel a distance of ten yards. Unless Black were to miss. Which he didn't. The bullet took Stapleton square in the chest. He fell back onto the floor. Black strode forward, fired another shot to the head. Stapleton spasmed, lay still.

The girl remained unconscious, despite the commotion. Black made his way round the operating table, crouched, searched Stapleton's pockets, found a set of keys. There were folded sheets on a shelf. Black got one, flapped it open, gently covering the girl, folding it round her, like a cocoon. He lifted her, held her close to his chest. He carried her out of the room, back along the corridor, past the devastation of rubble and debris, out the ragged hole created at the front of the building. He stood. He had no idea what to expect. But he was a clear target. He had nowhere else to go.

Four men approached, each armed.

Black cradled the girl tight. "This is why I came. For this girl, and more children inside. I plan to take them far from here. If you think it's worth killing me for this reason, then go ahead." Black's voice faltered, affected by a sudden wave of emotion. "She was to be murdered. None of you would know this. I came for these kids, because no one else would. I came because..." Black, through lack of sleep, through stress, through a wild range of feeling he could not begin to articulate, felt his voice crack. "...because I care."

The men looked at each other. What did they see? A man carrying a girl. No threat. No menace. Plus, with the devastation, they had bigger worries. Like the police. As if linked telepathically, they backed away, melting into the early morning gloom. Presumably to get back to the main hospital a mile off, and to their cars in the car park, then to drive the hell out, and leave the carnage behind them, and avoid the fallout.

Black had Stapleton's car keys in his hand. He made his way round to the car park at the side of the building. The girl groaned in his arms. There were only six parking bays, a car in each, including a 7-series BMW. Black pointed, pressed the unlock button. The car bleeped, lights flashed, the doors' locks clicked open. With great care, Black positioned the sleeping girl in a sitting position in the passenger's seat, buckled her up.

He went back, delicately picking his way through the wreckage, repeated the process, two little boys, placing them in the back seat beside their sister. He returned, for a final time, to the operating room, swept open the curtains, to Stapleton's theatre. On the table, a girl. She lay, still and pale as death. Black approached. She was breathing. She was alive. Black wrapped her in a sheet, left the ruined building, placed her in the back seat with her siblings, started the car, and eased out of the parking area, driving back the single road he had come.

It was 5.40am. For most, the beginning of a new day. Black saw no optimism or hope with the rising sun. He was weary to the bone. A darkness had settled in his soul. Never would he reach the bottom of the pit that was man's depravity. Its depth was endless.

He reached the main hospital, driving at a moderate speed. Surprisingly, there was no commotion. No panic. No police cars and flashing lights and congregations of frantic people. The car park was a little fuller. More lights were on. But the hospital still possessed that sleepy quality Black had experienced when he'd arrived. All was peaceful. All was good in the land of the sick. A million miles from the war zone a short distance away. The woods had absorbed most of the noise. What would staff and patients have heard? A few popping noises, like fireworks. What would they have seen, if they chose to look out the window? Nothing, Stapleton's miniature operating theatre invisible from the main hospital, shrouded in the gloom of thick trees.

The shit would hit the proverbial fan soon enough, thought Black. By which time, he would be long gone.

He passed the hospital, got to the main entrance. He knew the way back. A drizzle of rain started. The windscreen wipers started automatically. The sun's presence was fleeting, now swaddled in grey cloud. Looked like a dreary day, thought Black.

The girl in the front seat stirred. She cast a groggy eye at Black, gave a little smile.

"Finished now?" she said.

Black looked at her. Bustan had said they were from Syria. He doubted she knew little English. He knew no Arabic. Sometimes, you didn't need to talk, to communicate.

He returned the smile. "All finished."

He looked away, back to the road.

He wasn't finished. Not yet.

Words played and replayed in his mind.

All my fault.

54

Black drove back to Glasgow in silence. The kids were coming round, fidgeting in their seats, making small tired groans, as their bodies and minds returned to life. Fifty minutes later and once again he was in Govanhill, driving along Westmoreland Street. Black had no idea what to expect. He'd left a flat with a pile of dead bodies.

The place looked no different as he had left it, other than there were more parking spaces on each side of the road. Life went on, Black mused. People still went to work. The world didn't necessarily revolve round Adam Black and his adventures. He slowed, found a place, stopped opposite the main entrance to the block. He squinted up at the bay window on the top floor. The light was on. He saw a figure staring down. Looked like the mother.

"Stay here," he said quietly, not really knowing if they understood. He got out, locked the car, made his way inside, and up the stairs. He reached the top landing. The door was open. There, the mother and father. Behind them, in the shadows, Aksoy the interpreter.

The mother started speaking, voice high and desperate,

tugging Black's arm. Next to her, standing still and solemn, her husband.

Black gestured to Aksoy. "Come forward."

Aksoy sidled out from the hall. Black understood his reluctance. He'd seen Black kill his chums. If the kids were dead, what then would Black do? Aksoy waited, arms at his side, fingers twitching in little nervous flutters.

"Tell them their children are in the car outside. Tell them they're safe."

Aksoy drew a long exhalation. Black wondered how long he'd been holding his breath. He spoke. The mother listened, not for one second taking her eyes off Black. When Aksoy had finished, her shoulders crumpled, she cried soft tears. She leaned forward, hugged Black, crying into his shoulder.

He held her close.

"What now?" Aksoy asked.

Black didn't respond. He held on to the woman, soaking up all her pain and worry, as if by touch alone, he could remedy all her fears. Gently, he released her.

"We'll get the children. Then you'll phone the police, and you'll wait for them to arrive. You will explain what happened. These people were tricked by Bustan. You will interpret for them."

Aksoy stared at Black, his scrawny throat twitching with every swallow. He licked his lips, about to formulate a response. Black anticipated.

"How you deal with the police is your business. You have to take your chances. You can deny you knew what Bustan was doing. If they don't believe you, then get a good lawyer. I don't really give a shit. But you don't mention my name. And you stick with this family as long as you can, until they get proper representation. Do you hear me, Aksoy?"

Aksoy blinked, nodded. Black wasn't convinced. He had one

of the Berettas in his inside jacket pocket. He pulled it out, pointed it an inch from Aksoy's forehead. The man and woman gave a collective gasp.

"If you don't do as I ask, Aksoy, I'll find you and put a bullet in your brain. Your friends in the hall could testify to my skill in such matters. If they were able. You deserve to die a hundred times over. This way, you stay alive. You understand me?"

Aksoy's response was swift and unequivocal. "Yes."

Black tucked the semi-automatic back in his pocket. They followed him down the stairs, to Stapleton's 7-series parked opposite, far and away the best car on the street. The children were awake, but still drowsy. They gave weak smiles when they saw their parents. The mother opened the back door, unbuckled their seat belts, bundled the three in her arms. The father opened the passenger door, leant in, held his daughter. He was crying.

Black regarded Aksoy. "Phone the police. Now. On loudspeaker."

Without complaint, Aksoy tapped a number. A voice answered. *What service?*

He was referred to police emergency. *Four dead men.* He gave the address. *Come quickly.*

Black was satisfied. He reckoned a posse of cops would get there in about five minutes. He tossed the keys for the BMW at Aksoy. "Compliments of Dr Stapleton."

He left them, headed back to his own car, parked a hundred yards further down the street.

All my fault.

Three simple words, expressing a startling possibility. There had always been a niggle, a doubt, lurking in the shadowy corners of his mind. A niggle he had never explored. Never dared to explore.

Desmond Gallagher had been murdered. Both Malcolm

Copeland and Dr Michael Stapleton had denied their involvement, in situations when there was no legitimate reason for them to lie.

Black thought he had the answer. Three simple words.

As often happens, the truth had always been there, hiding in plain sight.

Black would have to return. To the beginning.

55

Deborah Gallagher's house looked quiet. The police had been and gone, presumed Black. Statements taken, Ringo and his friends escorted off the premises in handcuffs, and placed in the back of a police van. Tranquillity had returned. The bad guys departed. All was well in the sleepy hamlet of Thorntonhall, though doubtless the circumstances would be the source of much speculation and gossip for years to come.

Black parked his car in the driveway. He let himself into the house. He went through to the kitchen. The reception after the funeral seemed a million years ago. The bottles of wine. The neat display of food. The people there conversing in low solemn murmurs. The quiet, grave figure of Tony, the younger son, greeting Black in a formal dignified manner, way beyond his years. Face pale and pinched. A mixture of what? Confusion, sadness. And something else perhaps.

Sitting on the couch where Black had slept was Chris Gallagher. On the coffee table a glass cut from crystal, and in it, a liquid possessing the unmistakable colour of whisky.

Chris looked up. He smiled. "Adam. It's good to see you. I've been worried. We hadn't heard from you."

"You don't have to worry about me."

Chris gestured to the whisky. "Can I tempt you?"

"Not today."

He sat opposite. The windows allowed a wan listless morning light, casting shadows.

"The police have been?" Black asked.

"A troop of them. Ringo accepted his fate, I think. As you suggested, better for him in the long run."

"He'll do a stretch. He'll be out in six months. But he doesn't care about you. He presents no danger. Your mother, she's sleeping?"

Chris nodded, said nothing.

"All my fault," said Black suddenly.

Chris jerked his head up. "What?"

"Three words. I didn't give them much credence. Not at the beginning. Your brother wrote those words on a piece of scrap paper, before he swallowed a bottle of pills. You said the same thing, when you were cooking pasta. All my fault. It didn't register. But then I guess I had what you might describe as a revelation. Or perhaps a deduction. You said something. I didn't pick up on it. Not right away." He held Chris's stare. "But then I did."

Chris said nothing. He looked at Black, expression like cold marble.

"You told me your father was shot four times. How would you know that? It wasn't mentioned in the papers. It's not something the police would reveal. How would you know that, Chris?"

Chris picked up the glass, drank the contents, placed it back carefully on the table. "I think you already know how, Adam."

"I think I do. And I think I know why. The victims always feel they're to blame. But it isn't true. It's not your fault. Nor your brother's."

Chris's eyes brimmed with tears. "It started when I was maybe four of five. I can't remember exactly." He took a long breath, brought his hand to his mouth, bit into the knuckle. He closed his eyes. Bringing back the nightmare. "He crept into my bedroom, when Mum was asleep. Cuddles. He wanted cuddles."

Another deep ragged breath, stemming back more tears. "But it was so much more." He bowed his head, lowered his voice to a whisper. "It didn't stop. On and on. Relentless. He said if I told, no one would believe me. I'd be sent away." He looked up, glared at Black, almost accusingly. "He said everyone would call me a liar. A filthy little liar. He said it was all my fault."

"And your mother?"

Chris shook his head. "He was clever and devious. Aren't they always? She never knew. Quiet places. The dead of night. Again and again. It never stopped."

"But it did stop. For you."

"I was fourteen. It was like a tap, flowing all the time, then suddenly it switched off. My father became interested in..." He couldn't finish the sentence.

"In Tony," said Black.

Chris wrapped his arms round his chest, rocked back and forth. "I got out. Ran away. Joined the army. Leaving my little brother, alone, with him. I'm just a fucking coward. That's all I am. Just a fucking coward."

Black waited, said, "Then what happened."

"One evening, Tony phoned. He couldn't take it. He wanted to die. *He wanted to fucking die.* We cried. And then we plotted. It had to stop. The bastard was jogging every evening. We knew his route. I had a motorbike. I waited, got some leave, and rode up, booked into a cheap hotel in Glasgow. Tony phoned me when my father had left the house. He wasn't difficult to find. I passed him. I got off the motorbike, and shot him four times. I fucking killed him and left him on the road. Maybe God was smiling. I came, I went. No one saw me. You know what?"

Black said nothing.

"I didn't feel a fucking thing. No anger. No hatred. I was like a shell. An empty vessel. It was like killing a fucking fly. What does that make me?" He straightened, blinked, as if he'd been away, and just returned, taking stock of his surroundings. He looked at Black. "What will you do, Adam?"

Black chose his words carefully. "You and Tony will survive this. Your father scarred you. Deep scars. But scars heal, in time. Even the ones you can't see. What will I do? Nothing, because there's nothing to be done, other than tell you that you did the right thing. That it was never your fault. You killed him, and felt nothing. He didn't deserve anything more. He'd taken enough already. He'd taken everything. You killed a monster. And monsters deserve to die."

Black got up. Chris rose to his feet. Black reached out, held him. Chris gave way, and like the collapsing of a dam, wept.

Black had seen pain in all its forms, but none like this. He held him, not speaking. He absorbed the young man's suffering, bearing his grief, as if, by physical contact, the pain would lessen. Chris shuddered and sobbed, but the sobbing lessened, and eventually stopped. There were no more tears to shed. Chris stood back.

"Thank you, Captain Black."

"God speed, Chris."

Black left the house, left the village of Thorntonhall, and drove, with no particular destination in mind. The clouds had drifted, and the sun could be glimpsed, giving a brittle light.

He was bone weary. He knew however sleep would not come easy to him. He reflected on the last few days. Man's capacity for evil never failed to surprise, taking many forms, many shapes.

Like a million shadows, wavering under the surface of a still sea. If nothing else, he thought, mankind was inventive in the ways it wreaked horror. From the complex atrocities performed by devils like Stapleton and Canning, to brutal psychopaths like Malcolm Copeland. From the cheating deviousness of Charley Sinclair to the hidden atrocities perpetrated by Gallagher on his children.

And what then was he? What was Adam Black? A reflection of that horror? A different type of evil? A by-product of the devastation? Perhaps. The defining line between right and wrong was blurred. He had killed men – he adjusted his thoughts. He had *murdered* men. All for the pursuit of justice, the balancing of the scales. But he was motivated by more than that, and the notion whispered cold in his heart – he enjoyed the process. The killing. The havoc. He took a grim delight in the destruction of evil men. Which came at a price. Those around him he loved, ended up dead.

Black drove, sad and despondent, and wondered, as he often did, why the fuck he kept going.

He pushed the shadows away. He needed a whisky. He needed to forget.

The affair was over.

One month later

Black stood by the grave of a girl he never knew. A young beautiful girl, studying law, her life before her. A young girl who, bloodied and broken, had died in his arms, not understanding why. Nor indeed had he.

He laid a single rose. A robin flew down, suddenly, and landed on the headstone, dauntless, unafraid.

Hope?

Perhaps.

Black left the cemetery, back to his car, and like Chris, like the mother of the rescued children, like many others he had known, he cried.

EPILOGUE

FINALE

That which you sow does not come to life
Unless it dies.
— Corinthians 15-36

In a cabin built of timber, with a pitched roof of corrugated iron the colour of old blood, music played on a somewhat antiquated CD player. No one would hear Mick Jagger's drawl. Not here. The cabin sat solitary, by a broad stream, on the edge of nowhere, in the very north of Scotland. When it rained, the sound on the metal roof was like a thousand heartbeats. When it snowed, the world turned white.

In the distance, not far, the brooding wedge of rock that was Ben Hope. A great carcass of stone and ice, rising up from the peaty moors, immune from time and weather. In summer, despite the cold, the ground was bright with alpine flowers. Great swathes of colour. Purple, red and yellow, and a myriad of shades in between.

When he'd first seen the land, the colours, he thought of a winter jacket he'd bought his daughter. *Her rainbow jacket.* All bright and splendid. A splash of wonder. But in his dreams – his nightmares – the colours always morphed to red. Like the sunset. Like the corrugated roof above his head. The colour of old blood.

Here, in the heart of nowhere, no damage could be done. Here, the equation was simple. Just him, and his old friend. A friend who had been waiting a lifetime to embrace him. An embrace countless others had felt, including his wife and daughter.

Now, at last, he was prepared. It had come to this, and he was glad. Already, he could glimpse their faces. Their smiles. His heart sang. In the shadows, somewhere unseen, his friend waited. Patient as time. And he was glad of that too.

The cabin lacked everything but the most basic requirements. This was of no concern to him. On a table was an empty bottle of Glenfiddich. Beside it, a revolver loaded with a single bullet.

It was midday, the weather unsettled. Rain came down, in short light flurries. The sky was a canvass of black bruising. A downpour would follow shortly. The music stopped. For a brief moment, a stillness settled.

A deer nosed close to the front door, maybe looking for food. It jerked its head up suddenly, stiffened, sensing movement.

When the gunshot split the silence, it jerked away, and bounded off.

Then the rain started.

And the heavens opened.

Black stepped out, into the cold wet highlands, head dizzy with drink and took a deep calming breath, and thought, *Not today.*

THE END

ADAM BLACK WILL RETURN

A NOTE FROM THE PUBLISHER

Thank you for reading this book. If you enjoyed it please do consider leaving a review on Amazon to help others find it too.

We hate typos. All of our books have been rigorously edited and proofread, but sometimes mistakes do slip through. If you have spotted a typo, please do let us know and we can get it amended within hours.

info@bloodhoundbooks.com

Printed in Great Britain
by Amazon

33492131R00152